## Olivia didn't object to them all sharing the nursery.

She followed him upstairs to the room he'd set up for Cameron. Leo had purposely made it as identical as possible to the one at Olivia's so the boy would have some continuity.

Cameron didn't stir when Olivia put him in the crib, but neither Leo nor Olivia moved away despite the baby being sound asleep. They stood there several long moments, watching him, and Leo was pretty sure that, like him, Olivia was doing some prayers of thanks that their little boy hadn't been hurt.

"We need to find out who's behind the attack," she muttered.

Yeah, they did, and Leo intended to get started on that tonight. First, though, there was another matter they had to discuss. He took Olivia by the hand and led her to the other side of the room. Far enough for them to keep an eye on the baby but not so close to the crib as to wake him.

# TARGETING
# THE DEPUTY

---

USA TODAY Bestselling Author

## DELORES FOSSEN

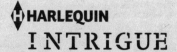

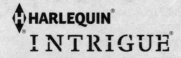

**HARLEQUIN®**
**INTRIGUE®**

Recycling programs
for this product may
not exist in your area.

ISBN-13: 978-1-335-48925-8

Targeting the Deputy

Copyright © 2021 by Delores Fossen

This edition published by arrangement with Harlequin Books S.A.

For questions and comments about the quality of this book,
please contact us at CustomerService@Harlequin.com.

Harlequin Enterprises ULC
22 Adelaide St. West, 40th Floor
Toronto, Ontario M5H 4E3, Canada
www.Harlequin.com

**Printed in U.S.A.**

**Delores Fossen**, a *USA TODAY* bestselling author, has written over one hundred novels, with millions of copies of her books in print worldwide. She's received a Booksellers' Best Award and an RT Reviewers' Choice Best Book Award. She was also a finalist for a prestigious RITA® Award. You can contact the author through her website at www.deloresfossen.com.

### Books by Delores Fossen

### Harlequin Intrigue

#### *Mercy Ridge Lawmen*

*Her Child to Protect*
*Safeguarding the Surrogate*
*Targeting the Deputy*

#### *Longview Ridge Ranch*

*Safety Breach*
*A Threat to His Family*
*Settling an Old Score*
*His Brand of Justice*

#### *The Lawmen of McCall Canyon*

*Cowboy Above the Law*
*Finger on the Trigger*
*Lawman with a Cause*
*Under the Cowboy's Protection*

### HQN

#### *Last Ride, Texas*

*Spring at Saddle Run*
*Christmas at Colts Creek*

Visit the Author Profile page at Harlequin.com.

## CAST OF CHARACTERS

*Deputy Leo Logan*—When someone tries to murder him and set up his ex to take the blame, he's drawn into an investigation that puts him, his ex and their son in danger.

*Olivia Nash*—Leo's ex who ended their relationship shortly after she learned she was pregnant with his child. But Olivia is keeping a secret that could be the reason someone now wants Leo and her dead.

*Cameron Logan*—Leo and Olivia's son. He's only a year old and has to be protected at all costs.

*Randall Arnett*—A local rancher who would go to any lengths to get back at Leo, who's investigating him for murder.

*Samuel Nash*—Olivia's father. He's wealthy, controlling and despises Leo, but is he the one who wants Leo dead?

*Bernice Saylor*—She's managed Samuel's estate for over twenty years, and it's possible she knows more than she's saying about the attempts on Leo's and Olivia's lives.

*Rena Oldham*—Samuel's longtime girlfriend who could have her own agenda for wanting Olivia and Leo out of the way.

# Chapter One

Deputy Leo Logan heard the movement behind him a split second too late. He whirled around, automatically reaching for his gun. But before he could draw it, he felt the pain slice over his arm.

He caught a glimpse of the knife. Another glimpse of the guy holding it. The man was wearing all black and had on a ski mask—also black. He was lunging with the knife to try to cut Leo again.

That gave Leo a major surge of adrenaline. And a hit of raw anger. He didn't know who the hell this idiot was, but Leo had no intention of just standing there while he stabbed him.

Leo ducked, avoiding the next slice, and in the same motion lowered his head and rammed right into the guy's gut. His attacker made a strangled sound, like a balloon dteflating. Leo had obviously knocked the breath out of him, but he took it one step further. He stood upright and plowed his fist into his attacker's face. The guy didn't fall but only staggered back, so Leo punched him again.

The man dropped to his knees on the ground, the knife clattering on the concrete next to him.

Leo heard another sound. Running footsteps behind him. He pivoted in that direction, this time managing to draw his gun. However, it wasn't the threat his body had geared up for. It was his brother.

Sheriff Barrett Logan.

It wasn't a surprise to see Barrett since this was the parking lot of the Mercy Ridge Sheriff's Office, but it was the last place Leo had expected to be attacked. It took a lot of guts, or stupidity, to come after a lawman on his own turf.

"What the hell happened?" Barrett snapped. He didn't wait for a response before he added, "Your arm's bleeding. Are you okay?"

Leo gathered his breath and tried to figure out the answer to his brother's question. He didn't think the wound was that deep, but it was already throbbing like a bad tooth. The knife had cut through his shirt, making a gash on his forearm. And there was blood. Thankfully, the wound wasn't gushing, but it was enough that he'd need it cleaned and bandaged.

"This moron attacked me," Leo growled.

As if he'd declared war on it, Leo kicked the knife away from the man, reached down and yanked off the ski mask. It was almost 6:00 p.m. but there was still plenty of light, so he had no trouble seeing the guy. Brown hair, brown eyes. Bulky build.

He was a stranger.

"Who are you?" Leo demanded, and that was just the first of many questions he had for this goon.

Barrett moved in to frisk him.

"I want a lawyer," the guy yelled.

Leo groaned. He didn't mind people exercising their civil rights, but this jerk hadn't minded violating Leo's rights by knifing him.

Barrett cuffed the man, dragging him to his feet. His brother took a wallet from the guy's pocket and handed it to Leo.

"Milton Hough," Leo relayed to Barrett. "He's got a San Antonio address."

Leo had known the guy wasn't local. Mercy Ridge was a small ranching town, and Leo had lived here his entire life. He knew every resident and vice versa, and he was certain he'd never laid eyes on Milton.

"I want a lawyer," Milton repeated, shouting now. "Call Olivia Nash, and she'll get one for me."

Despite his throbbing arm, that got Leo's full attention, and everything inside him went still. Unlike Milton Hough, that name was *very* familiar to Leo. In fact, Olivia was the mother of his one-year-old son, Cameron, and Leo and she were in the middle of a nasty custody battle.

One that Leo didn't want to believe had just gotten a whole lot nastier.

"Olivia?" Barrett questioned, his eyes meeting Leo's.

"Yeah," the thug verified. "Just get my phone out

of my jacket pocket. The last call I got was from her, so her number's on top."

"Right," Leo snarled. "And I'm to believe some idiot who'd attack a cop."

"Check the phone for yourself," Milton offered.

Leo debated it for a few seconds before he reached into Milton's jacket pocket and took out his cell. It felt as if he'd been clubbed again when he saw Olivia's name and number there.

*Hell.*

"Told you she called me," Milton said, and while his tone wasn't exactly a gloat, it was close.

Barrett certainly wasn't gloating. He was cursing and looking at Leo with a mountain of concern. "I'll book this guy. Go to the hospital, get your arm checked and then you can go see Olivia. You sure you're okay to drive? I can have the ambulance pick you up."

"I'm fine," Leo snapped.

He ignored the pain in his arm, got in his truck and drove away once Barrett had Milton inside the police station. There was a deputy and a dispatcher working this shift, so Barrett would have help if he needed it. Maybe Barrett would be able to find some answers, too, but Leo hoped to get a jump-start on that by seeing Olivia.

Olivia didn't live far, only a couple of miles away in the nearby town of Culver Crossing, so it only took Leo a few minutes before he pulled into the driveway of the Craftsman-style house. It was small and modest, not exactly the kind of place most folks would believe an *heiress* should live, but Olivia had bought it so that Cameron would be closer to Leo. The For Sale sign in front of it reminded him, though, of the rift between them.

Had that rift caused Olivia to go off the deep end and hire someone to hurt him? Or even kill him?

Leo didn't want to believe it. After all, he and Olivia had once been lovers. But they hadn't been in love. Not the kind of love that lasted anyway.

That was one of those "fine line" distinctions.

What they'd had was a short affair that had ended in her sudden breakup with him. When Leo had found out she was pregnant, Olivia hadn't denied it was his child, but she certainly hadn't done anything to remedy their breakup. And now she was challenging their agreement so she could move Cameron out of state.

Since his arm was still bleeding, Leo tore off his shirtsleeve and tied it around the gash like a makeshift bandage. That way, Cameron wouldn't see any blood. His little boy wasn't old enough to understand what'd happened, but he might be alarmed if he realized his dad had been injured.

Leo got out of his truck, went straight to Olivia's door and knocked. Impatience caused him to knock again just a few seconds later. He finally heard the locks being disengaged. The front door opened.

Olivia.

She clearly hadn't been expecting company because she was wearing jeans and a baggy T-shirt, and her dark brown hair was scooped up in a messy ponytail. Cameron wasn't with her. Under normal circumstances, Leo would have wanted to see his son, but he was thankful for some privacy. Privacy that he ensured by stepping inside and shutting the door behind him. Olivia didn't have any close neighbors on either side of her house, but there was one across the street.

"Oh my God, you're bleeding." Olivia's normally cool green eyes widened.

He ignored her and glanced around. "Where's Cameron? Is he with the nanny?"

She shook her head, her attention still on his arm. "He's asleep. He missed his afternoon nap and was so cranky that I went ahead and put him to bed early. I sent Izzie home."

Izzie Landon was the nanny, and while Leo liked the woman, he was glad she wasn't there, either.

"What happened?" Olivia asked.

"You tell me. Milton Hough." He threw the name out there and watched for any signs of recognition.

Leo didn't see any.

He wished he could say that he knew her well enough to know if she was hiding the truth, but he obviously wasn't a good judge when it came to Olivia. He definitely wouldn't have had an affair with her if he'd thought she was capable of sending a thug after him. And if she'd truly done that, there was no way in hell he was going to let his son stay another moment with her.

"Milton Hough?" she repeated, seeming genuinely confused. "Who is he?"

Leo continued to stare at her. "About ten minutes ago, he came after me in the parking lot of the sheriff's office. He had a knife and did this to me." He tipped his head to his injured arm.

Olivia opened her mouth. Closed it. Then she gasped. "This man tried to kill you?"

"Yeah." Leo dragged in a breath before he continued. "Then, as Barrett was arresting him, he cried for a lawyer and said I was to call you."

"Me?" she blurted out. "Why would he say that?"

"You tell me. I checked his phone, and you called him about a half hour ago."

"No." Olivia frantically shook her head. "I didn't."

"I saw your number in his phone," Leo argued, and had to tamp down the anger. However, he didn't tamp down his own confusion and his cop's instincts. Now that he was thinking straight, he had to ask himself why Olivia would have left any record of her contact with Milton if she'd hired the man to do him harm.

And the answer was—she wouldn't have.

"Show me your phone," he insisted.

Some of the color drained from her face. "I can't. I lost it. I don't know where, but I was going to drive into San Antonio in the morning and get a new one."

"You lost it," he mumbled and then silently cursed. Before Cameron had been born, that was profanity Leo would have said aloud, but he'd learned to tamp that down, too.

"Yes." Her breath swooshed out, and Olivia looked as if she might stagger back. Or even collapse. She didn't. She steeled herself and met him eye to eye. "Someone must have used my phone to call that man."

Leo could see that happening. Of course, that led him to the next question. Or rather, to a comment.

"Your father," was all he said.

Samuel Nash. He was a rich cattle broker, and he hated Leo for getting involved with Olivia, his precious daughter.

She shook her head again, denial all over her face. "You can't think my father's responsible," Olivia insisted.

Samuel had never had a friendly word for Leo, had always treated Leo like dirt, but it was still a stretch to believe the man was capable of something like this.

"When and where is the last place you saw your phone?" Leo persisted.

More of that color left her face and she hesitated for a long time. "I was at work in my office…at my father's."

It didn't surprise Leo that's where she'd last used

her phone. Olivia was often at her family's estate just outside San Antonio, and she did, indeed, have an office there where she ran her late mother's charity foundation.

"I didn't notice it was missing until I got home," she went on. "The pharmacy here had some of those no-contract phones and I bought one so I could call Bernice and have her look for mine."

Bernice Saylor, the household manager for the Nash estate, would have been a good person to contact. Well, good for Olivia anyway. Bernice had made it clear to Leo that she hated him as much as Samuel did. Apparently, Bernice didn't think her boss's daughter should have been slumming around with a small-town cop.

"Bernice couldn't find my phone," Olivia added. "But it's possible I dropped it somewhere. Maybe even here when I was getting out of my car."

Yeah, that was possible. But if that'd happened, it meant the person who'd found it had used it to set up Olivia, to make her look guilty of orchestrating the attack against him.

To the best of Leo's knowledge, there was no one in Mercy Ridge who had that kind of grudge against Olivia. But Milton might know for certain who'd hired him. Leo figured he was more likely to get a truthful answer from him than he would from Samuel or Bernice. Still, both of them would have to be questioned.

"You really need to have someone take a look at that arm," Olivia murmured.

When he glanced down at the makeshift bandage, Leo saw the fresh blood seeping through the cloth. Mercy. He might need stitches, after all. But there was an even bigger concern here.

"Look, I don't know what's going on," he admitted, "but if someone is setting you up, Cameron and you could be in danger."

That grabbed her attention. On a muffled gasp, Olivia pressed her hand to her throat. "You really believe that?"

"It's a possibility." He wouldn't sugarcoat this. "I don't want you two alone here tonight." Then he added what he knew Olivia wasn't going to like. "I'll stay with you."

He waited for her to object, and he could tell that's exactly what she wanted to do. Her father would give her all kinds of grief if he found out Leo had spent the night. But Leo didn't care a rat about that. He only needed to make sure his little boy stayed safe.

"You shouldn't be out driving anywhere tonight, either," Leo continued. That would nix any idea she got about going to her father's. "I also don't intend to get another deputy to do this. Cameron's my son, and I'm the one who should protect him."

Olivia finally nodded. "You can stay tonight."

Maybe it wouldn't take longer than that because Barrett would get the answers they needed from

Milton. If someone had actually hired Milton to attack Leo, he might give them the name if he were offered some kind of plea deal. Then Barrett could make an arrest and there wouldn't be any sort of threat to Olivia or Cameron.

"You still need someone to check your arm," Olivia reminded him.

Leo huffed, knowing she was right. He took out his phone and called the Culver Crossing Hospital. He requested an EMT come to Olivia's house. That way, he wouldn't have to leave her alone.

"How good is your security system?" Leo asked, putting his phone away.

"It's very good. My father had it set up for me when I moved here."

Of course, he had. Samuel was overly protective of Olivia in every possible way. Not just her safety but her personal life, too. Leo supposed that might have had something to do with Samuel losing his wife in a car accident when Olivia had only been ten. But the man crossed too many lines as far as Leo was concerned.

"Your father's got to be upset about me challenging you for custody." Leo threw the words out there, already knowing the answer. Yeah, Samuel would be upset. Olivia was, too.

"He is," she admitted, dodging his gaze now. "He doesn't want me to move to Oklahoma."

That was probably the only thing that Leo and Samuel agreed on. Well, that and their love for Cameron. Even though Samuel could be a hard-nosed SOB, Leo didn't doubt that the man loved his grandson.

"I'm not going to rehash all of this tonight," Olivia said, sounding a whole lot stronger than she had just seconds earlier. Leo could practically feel her digging in her heels.

They had indeed gone through all of this. Many times.

Olivia wanted to relocate to Tulsa to take over a nonprofit home and counseling center for troubled teens. She had an emotional connection to the center since it was something her mother had started twenty years ago, just months before her death. Leo couldn't dispute that it was a worthwhile cause, but he knew Olivia could run it from Culver Crossing, as she'd been doing for the past decade. Then, she wouldn't have to take Cameron out of state and to a place where Leo wouldn't be able to see him as often as he did now.

As much as Leo wanted to accommodate her on the no-rehashing, he had to know something. "Would Samuel do something to try to discredit you? Is he so pissed off at you over this move that he would try to take both of us out of the custody picture?"

There it was. All laid out for her.

"My father wouldn't do this," Olivia murmured, her voice shaky now.

Hell. There was enough doubt in her tone to confirm that her father was truly a suspect in this attack. He would need to pay Samuel a visit first thing in the morning.

Leo turned away from Olivia when he heard the vehicle come to stop outside her house. "It's probably the EMT. Stay back until I make sure."

That put a fresh round of alarm in her eyes, but Leo wasn't taking any chances. That's why he waited until Olivia had left the foyer and gone into the living room. He also put his hand over his weapon when he opened the door. The moment Leo did that, however, he heard a sound that he definitely didn't want to hear.

A gunshot.

## Chapter Two

The terror shot through Olivia, causing her heart to jump straight to her throat as she ran back to the foyer. Because she knew what she'd just heard. Knew what it meant.

Someone had just fired a shot at Leo.

Oh mercy. Someone was trying to kill him.

She latched onto his arm, yanking him deeper inside the house, but Leo was already moving in that direction. He slammed the door, locked it and then raced to the window in the living room that faced the front yard. Obviously, he had already geared up for a fight.

"Cameron," Olivia said, her son's name gusting out with her breath.

Leo didn't try to stop her when she started running to the rear of the house. Even if he had, she would have fought him off. She had to get to her son. She had to make sure he was okay, protect him.

She heard another shot just as she reached the nursery, but she didn't look back. Olivia rushed to the crib and, thanks to the night-lights in the room, she saw her baby. Asleep. Unharmed.

Safe.

The relief came like a flood, and she scooped him into her arms, brushing kisses on his cheeks and head. Cameron woke and made a fussy sound of protest at being disturbed. Olivia ignored that, too, and raced into the bathroom with him. She stepped into the shower stall where she hoped the tiles would stop any bullets from reaching them.

But the shots could definitely reach Leo.

That brought on a fresh round of terror. It didn't matter that he despised her. Didn't matter that they were at odds over this custody issue and her intended move. He was still Cameron's father, and she didn't want him hurt.

However, she did want to know why this was happening.

First, the knife attack by a man who claimed she'd called him. Now this. Olivia prayed they'd find out soon what was going on so they could put a stop to it.

When her lungs began to ache, she released the breath she'd been holding and continued to listen. No more gunshots, thank goodness, but she did hear Leo talking to someone. Maybe to someone on the phone.

"Olivia, are you and Cameron all right?" Leo called out to her several moments later.

"Yes," she managed to say. "I have him in the bathroom."

The sound of her voice caused Cameron to start fussing again. Olivia tried to rock him so that he'd go back to sleep. If he was awake, he might pick up on her tense muscles and therefore her fears.

Olivia heard the footsteps and, even though she knew it was probably Leo, she turned Cameron away from the door, putting her body between him and anyone who might enter. But the person who came in was Leo.

He looked like a fierce warrior with his black hair and stone-gray eyes. Tall, rangy and ready for battle. The anger was coming off him in thick waves that she could practically see. But for once that particular emotion wasn't aimed at her.

"The shooter sped off. I couldn't go after him," he said, though she wasn't sure how he could speak with his jaw muscles set so hard.

"No," she quickly agreed. Because that would have meant leaving Cameron and her alone. Olivia didn't have a gun and wouldn't have wanted to face down an armed man when she had Cameron to protect. "Did you see who it was?"

He shook his head and moved closer, his attention on Cameron. Thankfully, the baby had gone back to sleep on Olivia's shoulder. Leo leaned in—so close that she caught his scent—and brushed a kiss on top of the boy's head.

Olivia looked away, unable to make herself resistant to Leo. She'd never managed to do that. But she had plenty of reasons why she couldn't give in to the flickers of heat he caused in her body.

"I locked the front door and then called the Culver Crossing PD," Leo said, gently brushing his fingers over Cameron's hair. Hair that was identical in color to Leo's. Ditto for her son's eyes. "Sheriff Jace Castillo will be here in a few minutes. It's his jurisdiction," he reminded her, not sounding very happy about that.

Olivia knew the reason for that unhappiness. There was bad blood between the Castillos and the Nashes because, several decades ago, Leo's mother had had an affair with Jace's father, and it had ripped both families apart. Olivia was well aware of how some events from the past could affect the present.

Not in a good way, either.

"I'm surprised you didn't call Della instead," she murmured. Since Della was a Culver Crossing deputy sheriff and also his soon-to-be sister-in-law, Leo would have no doubt found her easier to deal with.

"I heard my brother mention that Della had just finished a long shift. Besides, Jace would have had to come in on something like this anyway."

Yes, because what had happened was so serious—the attempted murder of a police officer. And not the first attempt tonight, either.

Sweet heaven, what was going on?

"We'll wait in here until Jace arrives." Leo

moved in front of her then, taking up the stance to protect them both if someone made it into the house and came through the bathroom door.

"All the windows and the back door are locked," she told him.

Olivia was certain of that because it was something she did even in the daytime. Cameron was walking now, and he was fast. She hadn't wanted to risk him getting outside the house. But she'd never thought it was something she'd need to do to keep out a would-be killer.

"I locked the front door," he added. Leo paused, the muscles stirring in his jaw again. "The shooter fired at the house." There was fresh anger in his voice now and in his eyes. "I don't think the bullets got through the walls, but they could have. *They could have*," he repeated in a hoarse mumble.

Olivia also felt plenty of anger, but it was beneath the fear and the question. "Did that man, Milton Hough, escape and do this?"

"No. I called Barrett, too, and he still has Milton in custody."

Normally, she would have considered that a good thing, but in this case it meant there were two attackers. At least. It also meant whoever had done this had no regard for the safety of a child.

"Who would have done this?" Olivia came out and asked. When he didn't give her an immediate answer, she added. "And it wasn't me."

"I know it wasn't you. No way would you have put Cameron at risk."

That stung. Because while it was true about Cameron, she wouldn't have put Leo in harm's way, either. In fact…well, she didn't want to go there. Not when she had other questions and concerns.

"Is this maybe connected to one of your investigations?" she suggested.

He opened his mouth but didn't get a chance to say anything because there was a knock at the door.

"It's me, Sheriff Castillo," Jace called out.

"Wait here," Leo instructed her, his weapon drawn as he left the bathroom and closed the door behind him.

Olivia held her breath again. She didn't suspect Jace of being behind the shooting, but the gunman could still be outside somewhere, waiting for Leo to answer the door so he could fire more shots at him.

Thankfully, she didn't hear any gunfire. Just the murmurs of a conversation between Jace and Leo, followed by footsteps. Several moments later, Leo opened the bathroom door. He came in, but Jace stayed in the doorway.

Even though the men weren't saying anything to each other, Olivia could feel the tension. She hoped that wouldn't stop them from working together on this because she was going to need all the help she could get.

"Are you okay?" Jace asked her.

Olivia nodded, but it was a lie. She was far from

being okay. "Did you see the man who shot into the house?"

"No," Jace answered. "But I'm going outside now to have a look around. I want Leo to stay in here with the baby and you, if that's all right."

Jace obviously knew about the custody battle. Heck, everyone in Mercy Ridge and Culver Crossing did. And Jace was clearly concerned that she wouldn't be comfortable with Leo being around her. She was uncomfortable, but that would skyrocket if she had to stay inside alone with Cameron.

"Leo should stay," she agreed.

Jace gave her a nod and shifted his attention to Leo. "You said the shooter's vehicle was a late-model pickup truck, either dark blue or black?"

"That's right. He was behind the wheel when he fired the shots, and he sped off after firing two rounds. I couldn't make out the license plate."

"And you're sure it was a man?" Jace pressed.

"Yeah. He had wide shoulders and beefy arms, and he was wearing a ski mask, just like the guy who attacked me earlier in Mercy Ridge."

That tightened Olivia's stomach even more. Someone had sent two men after Leo tonight, and both had used what could have been deadly force.

"After I've had a look around, I'll need to talk to both of you again," Jace said, sounding all cop. "I'll need statements. I'll also want you to tell me who you believe would do something like this, so be thinking about that while I'm gone."

Leo made a sound of agreement but, judging from his stony expression, it was a hard pill for him to swallow to be taking orders from a fellow cop. One he didn't especially like.

When Jace left, Leo stood in the bathroom doorway so he could look out into the hall. Keeping watch. Olivia tried to help by focusing on what Jace had told her to do—think about who had done this. She wished she could draw a blank, but she couldn't.

"Bernice." She hadn't intended to say that aloud, yet it was the first name that came to mind.

Leo looked back at her. "You think your father's household manager could have done this?"

"No. Not really." Flustered, she shook her head and wished she'd kept her mouth shut. "But she's upset about our custody fight. Upset with *you*," Olivia amended.

Leo certainly couldn't dismiss the possibility of Bernice's involvement. The woman could be overbearing, and she was fiercely loyal to Olivia's father. That meant Bernice was also upset with Olivia's move to Oklahoma.

"Bernice wouldn't have put Cameron in danger," Olivia stated. She would have added more to try to convince him about that, but his phone rang.

"It's Barrett," he relayed and, much to Olivia's surprise, put the call on speaker.

"How are things there?" Barrett immediately asked.

Leo took a deep breath before he answered. "No sign of the shooter. And Sheriff Castillo is on scene."

The sound that Barrett made conveyed both his sympathy and concern. Yes, there was definitely still bad blood between Jace and the Logan brothers.

"Milton clammed up," Barrett said a moment later. "He's waiting for a lawyer to drive over from San Antonio. Probably waiting for the DA to offer him some kind of plea deal, too."

"Hell," Leo muttered after he glanced at Cameron. No doubt to make sure he was still asleep. He was. "The shooter could have hurt my son." There was plenty of raw emotion in his voice.

"Cameron's okay?" Barrett asked.

"Yeah. It needs to stay that way. That's why I want to know if someone hired Milton and this other thug who fired into Olivia's house. I'll need the person's name, and if the two weren't hired, I have to know why they took it upon themselves to try to kill me."

"I want that, too," Barrett verified. "We might not need to deal with Milton, though. I'm getting a warrant to go over his financials to see if I can find a money trail. Then I might be able to figure out who paid him to do this. I'll also try to get his medical records."

That got Olivia's attention.

Obviously, it got Leo's, too. "Medical records?" he questioned.

Barrett paused again. "I found a bottle of prescription meds in Milton's pocket, and I looked it up. It's something that's given to patients with severe psychological disorders."

Olivia tried to process that. Maybe there'd been no hired guns. Just a mentally ill man who'd attacked Leo. Of course, that didn't explain the person who'd fired the shots outside her house, but it was a start.

"Where's my daughter?" someone shouted. "I want to see Olivia now!"

She groaned because she easily recognized that voice. Her father. And his being here definitely wasn't going to make things better.

"I need to make sure Cameron and Olivia are all right," her father went on. "If somebody shot at her, I want to see for myself that they weren't hurt."

"I have to go," Leo said to Barrett. Obviously, he also knew her father was there, and he ended the call.

"I told you that Olivia and your grandson are fine," she heard Jace say. The sheriff sounded just as annoyed as Leo looked.

But Olivia was past the mere annoyed stage. Why had her father come? Better yet, how had he known about the shooting? Her neighbors didn't know her dad well enough to have his phone number.

Moments later, Samuel stepped into the doorway of the bathroom. He was tall, bulky and imposing, a bouncer's build. And somehow his iron-gray hair didn't make him look old, only more formidable.

As usual, her father was wearing a suit, a dark gray one this time, and he had a gold sycamore leaf pin on his classic red tie. The pin was the symbol of his estate, Sycamore Grove, and he didn't just wear the emblem, it was also on the iron gates that fronted the house, on the vehicles' license plates. Even on the front door.

Jace was right behind Samuel, and Leo didn't budge to let her father come any closer to her. However, Olivia stepped closer because she wanted to see her father's expression when she asked him the questions that were causing the anger to ripple through her.

"Were you having me watched?" Olivia demanded. Cameron stirred and she patted his back to try to soothe him. She definitely didn't want her son to hear any part of this conversation. "Is that how you found out about the shooting?"

Maybe it was her steely tone, but her father flinched as if she'd slapped him. Of course, he could have reacted that way to make her feel sorry for what she'd just said. But Olivia didn't feel sorry for him.

"No, I'm not having you watched." Her father's voice was tight now, and his eyes were slightly narrowed. "I got an anonymous text, saying that Cameron and you had been attacked. I tried to call you several times. When I didn't get an answer, I drove straight here."

Since Olivia's replacement phone was in the kitchen and set to vibrate, she wouldn't have heard the calls, but the other part of his explanation didn't make sense.

"An anonymous text?" She sounded skeptical because she was. Olivia huffed. "Look, if you had someone spying on me, then that person saw the shooter. You need to give your watchdog's name to Sheriff Castillo and Leo so he can help them find this gunman."

At the mention of Leo's name, her father slanted him a glare. Leo glared right back.

"Do you have a watchdog around here?" Leo demanded.

Her father's glower got significantly worse. "No. I got a text, like I said. And you have no right to question me."

"I have the right." Jace jumped in. "If you know anything about the shooting, I want to hear it."

Samuel ignored Jace and stared at her.

"Leo." Her father spat the name out like venom. "He's the one you should be doubting and questioning. Go ahead—ask him. Have him tell you what this is all about."

Everything inside Olivia went still. "What do you mean?"

Her father didn't actually smile, but it was close. "Leo's the reason Cameron and you could have been killed. This is all his fault."

## Chapter Three

After dealing with Samuel for the past two years, Leo knew he shouldn't be surprised by the accusation. But there was something in Samuel's expression that had Leo wondering if there was any truth to it.

Olivia was already moving forward, but Leo motioned for her to stay back. It was somewhat of a miracle that Cameron was still asleep, and Leo didn't want him closer in case this *conversation* got loud. That was always a possibility when dealing with Samuel Nash.

"You actually believe these two attacks were my fault?" Leo questioned.

Samuel jabbed his index finger at Leo. "You bet they were. Because of your botched investigation, Randall Arnett is a free man and now he wants to get back at you."

Leo had wondered how long it was going to take for Randall's name to come up. He'd already considered it. But what Samuel had just said was a mix of truth and lies. Randall wasn't behind bars, but Leo hadn't botched the investigation into the man's missing girlfriend. Simply put, there hadn't been enough evidence to charge Randall.

"Randall threatened you," Samuel reminded him.

"Yeah, over a year ago," Leo verified. What he wouldn't say was that he'd been keeping close tabs on Randall, looking for anything he could use to prove the man's wrongdoing. "It'd be stupid for Randall to come after me like this," Leo added.

Samuel shrugged. "That doesn't mean he didn't. The person who texted me said Randall was responsible for the shooting. I can show you. It's right here." He took out his phone, holding up the screen for Leo to see.

"'Get to your daughter's place now,'" Leo read aloud. "'There's been a shooting. Dig into Deputy Leo Logan's case files if you want to know who pulled the trigger.'"

So, the person who'd sent that text hadn't specifically mentioned Randall. Interesting. Interesting, too, that Samuel had jumped to that conclusion.

"How exactly did you know about Randall Arnett?" Leo asked.

Samuel blinked, maybe surprised by the question. But he shouldn't have been. He should have known that was something Leo would press, especially since the man didn't live in Mercy Ridge and wouldn't necessarily be privy to the town talk about Randall.

"I make it a point to know what you're doing because it affects my daughter and grandson," Samuel insisted.

Olivia huffed. "You've been digging into Leo's investigations. You're looking for something you can use against him in the custody case."

Bingo. Leo was glad Olivia had realized her father would do something like this. The man fought dirty. Maybe dirty enough to stir up Randall to get him to launch an attack?

Maybe.

It was definitely something Leo would look into.

Samuel shifted his attention to Olivia. "You know I only want what's best for Cameron and you. I have to keep you safe. That's why you'll need to come home with me. Look at Leo's arm, at his gunshot injury. Something worse could happen to Cameron and you if you stay around him."

And there was another *bingo*. Samuel would use this shooting and anything else he could come up with to get Olivia and Cameron under his roof.

Exactly where Samuel wanted them.

"No," Olivia said before Leo could tell her that he thought it was a bad idea. The shooter could follow Olivia there, and while her father likely knew how to use a gun, he wasn't trained in law enforcement.

Samuel sighed. "I know you're upset. And scared. But you can't stay here. The man who fired those shots could come back."

Now, Leo did manage to speak first. "Olivia

and Cameron won't be staying here. But they'll be placed in protective custody until I can figure out what's going on."

Leo was surprised that lightning didn't bolt from Samuel's eyes. "Your protective custody?" he questioned as if that were a stupid idea.

"Either mine or Sheriff Castillo's." Leo hoped that, despite their differences, Jace would back him up.

He did. "Olivia and Cameron definitely won't be staying here," Jace agreed. "This is now a crime scene, and the grounds need to be processed. I've already called in a CSI team to look for tracks and spent shell casings. While that's going on, Olivia needs to be in a safe place, and Leo should be the one to decide where that safe place will be."

"Leo and Jace are right," Olivia said.

Her voice sounded strong but was edged with nerves. That was expected, Leo supposed, though he thought he detected something else beneath the surface. Maybe her father and she had had some kind of disagreement. If so, it probably had something to do with the move she wanted to make to Oklahoma. Samuel wouldn't want Olivia that far away from under his thumb.

"You'll go with Leo?" her father snarled.

She nodded, swallowed hard. "And before you tell me all the reasons why that shouldn't happen, remember this. Leo is Cameron's father and he'll do anything to protect his son."

"So will I," Samuel howled.

This time Cameron didn't just stir. The boy let out a loud wail, the sound tugging at Leo's heart. Samuel's shout had scared him.

Shooting a scowl at Samuel, Leo went to Olivia, who was trying her best to soothe the baby. However, the moment that Cameron spotted Leo, he reached out for him and babbled, "Dada." That tugged at Leo's heart, too, and he took Cameron into his arms.

"It's all right, buddy," Leo whispered to him and brushed a kiss on the top of his head.

Jace's phone buzzed. The sheriff gave each of them a long look, as if deciding whether or not he should leave them alone while he took the call. He must have decided a fight wouldn't break out because he stepped into the hall.

"You're a fool to trust him," Samuel immediately said to Olivia.

Leo didn't have to guess that Samuel was talking about him. Definitely no trust between them. But what did surprise Leo was his glimpse of a flicker of distrust in Olivia's eyes.

"I'd be a fool not to do what it takes to keep my son safe," Olivia countered.

Samuel huffed, and Leo decided if the man raised his voice this time, he would give him the boot. Cameron had been upset enough without adding more shouting to the mix.

"You can be safe with me," Samuel said, staring

at Olivia. No shouting. In fact, his voice leveled and took on a pleading tone. "I need you home. I'll be sick with worry over Cameron and you."

Olivia's expression and posture stayed stiff as she moved closer to Leo and stroked her hand down Cameron's back. That put Leo arm to arm with Olivia. A sort of united front against her father.

Something that wouldn't last.

Olivia always caved to Samuel.

"You know this is already a tough time for me," Samuel added a moment later.

"Because of Mom," she muttered.

Leo knew it was a tough time for Olivia, too. The anniversary of her mother's death was in a couple of days, and it would no doubt stir up some bad memories. Olivia had been just ten when her mom, Simone, had been killed in a car accident. Olivia had been in the car with her, trapped inside, while she watched her mother die.

Yeah, it would be bad.

And now it'd be worse because of this attack tonight. No way to push aside the sounds of those shots that'd been fired into the house.

Leo wanted to put his arm around Olivia, to try to comfort her. That was his kneejerk reaction any-way. Not only wouldn't she welcome that, it also wasn't smart. After all, they weren't exactly friends right now.

"You shouldn't have been in the car with Simone that night," Samuel muttered, and it seemed as if he was lost in the grief. "You shouldn't have had to go through that."

Olivia cleared her throat, her gaze shifting to meet Leo's. She was certainly a puzzle tonight because he wasn't sure what he was seeing there. Maybe, though, it was just the start of an inevitable adrenaline crash.

"Come home with me," Samuel insisted. The plea was gone, probably because he didn't like all the eye and arm contact she was making with Leo.

"No," she said, and repeated it when she turned back to her father. "No. And I need you to leave now."

The muscles tightened in Samuel's jaw, and Leo didn't think he was mistaken that the look the man gave his daughter was a borderline glare. A glare that Samuel would have likely added some venomous words to if Jace hadn't come back into the room.

Jace stopped, eyeing them all again. "A problem?" Jace asked.

"No," Olivia quickly answered. She began to stuff some diapers, clothes and toys into a large diaper bag. "I've already explained to my father that I'll be taking Cameron to Leo's."

Jace nodded, though he didn't seem convinced about Olivia's denial.

Neither was Leo. Something other than the obvious was wrong here.

"I need to go by the sheriff's office in Mercy Ridge," Jace told Leo. "I have to see Milton. But I'm in my cruiser, so I can take Olivia and you to your place first. I can go through it, too, just to make sure no one had tried to break in. Once you're there, the EMTs can have a look at that arm."

It was a generous offer, and it would free up Barrett from having to send out a deputy for backup duty.

"Cameron has a car seat in my truck," Leo explained. "I'll need to drive that, but I'd appreciate it if you'd make sure we get safely back to my ranch." He paused. "I'll want to question Milton, too, but I don't want to take Cameron there."

"I'll let your brother know what's going on," Jace assured him.

"Olivia," Samuel said, "reconsider this."

"No." She didn't hesitate, either. "Give me a minute to pack a bag," she added to no one in particular and hurried out of the room.

Samuel immediately turned to Leo. "You can convince her not to go to your house."

Leo gave him what he was certain was the flattest look in the history of flat looks. "Leave, Samuel," Leo insisted, making sure it sounded like an order from a cop. He'd had enough tonight and didn't want to deal another second with this man who'd tried to make his life a living hell.

Samuel shifted as if he might make that plea to Jace, but Jace managed a darn good flat look of his own. Leo didn't know how well the two men knew each other, but there didn't seem to be any tinge of friendliness.

"You're not going to take my daughter and grandson away from me," Samuel snarled to Leo, and with that, he finally headed out of the house.

"I'll lock the door behind him," Jace offered.

"Thanks," Leo muttered. He didn't want to take Cameron near an unlocked door until it was time to leave.

Leo fired off a quick text to his head ranch hand, Wally Myers, to alert him to be on the lookout for the shooter and to also patrol the grounds. Wally lived in the bunkhouse, along with two other hands, and Leo knew he could count on them to make sure the place was as safe as it could be.

Maybe that would be enough.

Olivia was true to her word about only taking a minute to pack a bag. She hurried back into the room, glanced around and seemed to take a breath of relief when she saw that her father wasn't there.

She hoisted her bag over one shoulder and put the filled diaper bag over the other. What she was also doing was avoiding eye contact with him. He would have called her on that, but Jace returned.

"There's no sign of the shooter," Jace said, "but I'd like to get Olivia and the baby inside the vehicle as fast as we can."

Olivia made a sound of agreement, and Leo handed Cameron back to Olivia. He also took her bag. As she'd done, he looped it over his shoulder to free up his shooting hand. He prayed it wouldn't be necessary, though, to do any firing. Not with his baby so close that he could be hurt.

"I want to see Milton, too," Olivia said as they made their way to the door. "I want to see if I recognize him."

There were safer ways for her to take that look. Leo fired off a quick text to Barrett to let him know they were leaving and to ask him to send a photo of Milton.

"Stay close to me," Leo instructed her, using his key fob to unlock his truck.

And he sucked in his breath, holding it.

Praying.

He fired glances all around but didn't see a gunman. Of course, the guy probably wouldn't just stand out in the open, not with two lawmen around. Still, the guy had been gutsy enough to launch an attack.

Jace moved when they did, and Leo and the sheriff kept Olivia and Cameron between them as they hurried outside and got into the truck. The moment Jace shut the passenger's-side door, he hurried over to his cruiser. Leo only waited long enough for Olivia to strap Cameron into his seat before he took off.

"Keep watch," Leo told her. He also wanted to tell her to get down on the seat so that she'd be out of harm's way, but he needed her eyes. If she could spot any signs of trouble, it could help him avoid being the target of more gunfire.

He hoped.

Right now, Leo was hoping a lot of things. He needed to catch the idiot who'd put Cameron and Olivia in danger, but he didn't want that to happen with his little boy around.

"Later," he said, giving her a heads-up, "I'll want to know what's going on between you and your father."

He'd figured Olivia would dole out a quick denial that anything was going on. But she stayed silent.

Hell.

Whatever this was, it had to be bad. Then again, things were rarely good when it came to Samuel. Leo wanted to know if her move to Oklahoma had anything to do with this father-daughter rift or whatever the heck it was.

His phone dinged. Rather than take his eyes off the road, he passed it to Olivia.

"It's from Barrett," she said. "It's a picture of Milton."

Thinking Barrett had gotten that photo rather fast, Leo made a quick glance at the screen. It was Milton's DMV photo.

"I don't recognize him," Olivia muttered. "I swear, I didn't hire him to kill you."

Leo had thought they'd already hashed this out. Apparently not. "Yeah, I got that."

And he left it at that. Because a conversation about a would-be killer could be a huge distraction, too.

Cameron made a fussy sound that caught Leo's attention. He never wanted to hear his boy cry, but such a sound now could drown out other things that he needed to be hearing. But the one fuss was it. While Leo drove on, the baby thankfully drifted back to sleep.

He heard Olivia make what he realized was a sigh of relief and, like him, she continued to keep watch as he drove. It wasn't a long trip, less than twenty minutes, but each mile felt as if it took an eternity. Leo didn't relax, however, when he pulled into his driveway. He did more glancing around, making sure there were no signs of an attacker. Nothing. And he hoped it stayed that way.

He spotted Wally at the side of the house. The ranch hand was carrying a rifle, but he gave Leo a welcoming nod, an assurance that all was well. Good. Leo pulled into his garage, but he didn't get out. He waited for Jace to join them and then shut the garage door to give them some extra cover.

"I can pause my security system with my phone," Leo explained as he pulled up the app.

No sensors had been triggered. That was the good news. The bad news was that no security system was foolproof.

"Wait here with Olivia," Leo instructed Jace once they were inside the mudroom. "I can go through the place faster than you can."

And *fast* would be key. Leo didn't want to be away from Olivia and Cameron any longer than necessary. That's why he drew his gun and started hurrying through the rooms—all twelve of them—checking each window, door and closet. He even looked under the beds and turned on all the lights as he went. That would help to illuminate the grounds, but it would also prevent a potential attacker from knowing which room they were in.

Leo had been raised in this house. The home that had once belonged to his parents before things had fallen apart. Before his mother had left them and his father had committed suicide. There were plenty of bad memories here. Plenty of really good ones, though, too. Right now, he needed to make sure nothing else bad happened to add to what had already taken place tonight.

While he made his way downstairs, he texted Wally again to instruct him to continue to keep watch. It'd be a long night for all of them, but any and all precautions were necessary.

"It's okay," Leo immediately told Jace and Olivia when he joined them in the mudroom. He looked at Jace. "Thanks."

Jace nodded. "I'll let you know if I find out anything about Milton."

Leo muttered another thanks and locked the front door when Jace left. He also reset the security system.

"We're staying in the nursery tonight," Leo insisted. "All three of us. You can take the sleep chair." It was an oversize recliner that Leo had used plenty of times himself when Cameron had stayed nights with him.

Olivia didn't object to them all sharing the nursery. She followed him upstairs to the room he'd set up for Cameron. Leo had purposely made it as identical as possible to the one at Olivia's so the boy would have some continuity.

Cameron didn't stir when Olivia put him in the crib, but neither Leo nor Olivia moved away despite the baby being sound asleep. They stood there several long moments, watching him, and Leo was pretty sure that, like him, Olivia was silently uttering some prayers of thanks that their little boy hadn't been hurt.

"We need to find out who's behind the attack," she whispered.

Yeah, they did, and Leo intended to get started on that tonight. First, though, there was another matter they had to discuss. He took Olivia by the hand and led her to the other side of the room. Far enough for them to keep an eye on the baby but not so close to the crib as to wake him.

"Okay..." Leo started, "want to tell me what's going on between you and your father?"

She dragged in a long breath, opened her mouth then closed it as if she'd changed her mind about what she was going to say. A few seconds crawled by before she finally spoke.

"I think my father might be a killer."

## Chapter Four

*I think my father might be a killer.*

The moment Olivia heard what she'd said, she wished she could take it back. This was definitely not something she should have brought up tonight, not when Leo and she were still recovering from the shock of the attack. In fact, she shouldn't have dropped the bombshell at all unless she had some proof to back it up.

She didn't.

But what she did have was a tightness in her chest and stomach. An unsettling feeling that what she'd said was the cold, hard truth.

Leo's eyes narrowed and he gave her a cop's stare. "You're going to need to explain that," he demanded.

Since there was no way Olivia would be able to dodge answering him, she gathered her breath and hoped this didn't blow up in her face. After all, Leo and she were in a custody battle, and he might be willing to use this against her.

"I got the police report of my mother's car accident," Olivia explained. "I read it, and I couldn't stop thinking about it."

Dreaming about it, too. The nightmares hadn't been as bad as actually witnessing her mother die. Nothing could have been that bad. But the nightmares had definitely shaken her.

"You hadn't read the report before?" Leo asked, no doubt hoping to spur her into continuing with her explanation.

"No. I didn't think reading it would help. It didn't," she added in a murmur. "There were drugs in my mom's tox screen. A combination of sleeping pills and amphetamines. I don't remember my mother ever taking either of those. Just the opposite. She was sort of a health nut and didn't even take over-the-counter pain meds when she had a headache."

Leo stayed quiet a moment, obviously processing that. "You think your father gave her those drugs?"

Olivia met his gaze. She wanted to shake her head again, wanted to erase all the doubts and worries about her dad having some part in this. But she couldn't.

"They were arguing a lot, and I heard my mom tell him that she wanted a divorce," she went on. "My dad might have drugged her out of anger. *Might*." She gave emphasis to the word, then groaned. "He wouldn't have done that, though, if he'd known I was going to be in the car."

"You sneaked into the car," Leo stated when she stopped. "Neither your mom nor your dad knew you were in the back seat. Isn't that right?"

Even though it was a question, Leo knew the answer. When they'd been lovers, she'd poured out her heart to him. No. Her parents hadn't known she'd been in the vehicle. After yet another argument, she'd heard her mother tell her father that she was packing her things and leaving. She hadn't heard her mom say anything about taking her along, though, so Olivia had hurried to the garage and gotten down on the floor behind the driver's seat. Her mother had only discovered her seconds before the crash.

"Right," she verified. "The drugs definitely affected my mother's driving. I remember her weaving on the road, and that's when I lifted my head and asked her if everything was okay."

It hadn't been okay at all and, within minutes, her mother was dead. The crash had injured Olivia, too, but in the grand scheme of things, a broken arm and bruises had been minor, especially considering she hadn't been wearing a seat belt.

"Where was your mom going that night?" he asked. "Did she say?"

"She didn't say specifically, only that she needed some fresh air and was going for a drive to try to clear her head. But I remember her telling my dad that she'd be filing for a divorce, that she'd had enough."

Leo continued to study her as if trying to pick apart every nuance of her expression. She didn't dare do the same to him. Best to avoid eye contact. Other kinds of contact, as well. Olivia didn't consider herself stupid; she'd felt the old attraction still simmering between them. An attraction that even an unplanned pregnancy and a custody battle couldn't cool. She couldn't play with that kind of fire again. It was too dangerous.

"You said your father could have drugged your mother out of anger," Leo said. "Had he done anything like that before?"

"Not that I know of. I don't remember him ever hitting her, either. They just argued a lot."

Leo touched his fingers to her chin, turning her head and forcing the very eye contact she was trying to avoid. And there it was. More than just a flutter of heat. The flash of it through her body. Leo had always been able to do that to her. Still could.

Olivia stepped back, away from his touch. But it didn't stop the need he'd stirred inside her. However, his expression helped with that. Obviously, he wasn't thinking about sex tonight. Nope. She was certain his expression was the same one he used when interrogating suspects.

"Why do you think your father might have had some part in the car accident?" he asked.

She seriously doubted the answer she'd give him would convince him that her father was guilty. Or that she was telling Leo the whole truth—which she wasn't. But she tried anyway.

"Because my father keeps bringing it up," she said. "For the past couple of weeks, he keeps telling me how sorry he was that I was in the car. Maybe it's just because of the anniversary of mom's death, but there seems to be more."

"*More?* You mean like guilt?" he pressed.

"Exactly like guilt," she confirmed. So, maybe Leo would understand her gut feeling, after all. "When I ask for more details of that night, he dodges the questions. Not hard questions, either. I asked him why they were arguing and wanted to know if Mom had threatened to leave him before."

Leo mumbled some profanity under his breath. "I'm betting he didn't like that."

"No." In fact, her father had stormed off during one of those conversations. The man definitely had a temper, and that hadn't been the first time she'd seen flashes of it. Many times, he'd aimed his temper at Leo.

"I also talked to Bernice," Olivia continued. "I asked her point-blank if my father could have had any part in that car accident, and she said absolutely not."

"Did she have an explanation for your mother's tox screen results?" Leo asked.

"None other than she was positive my father wasn't responsible. Of course, the woman idolizes him, so she probably wouldn't rat him out. The only reason I brought up the subject to her was that I thought I'd be able to read her expression if she thought there was any hint of wrongdoing on his part."

Again, Leo went quiet for several moments. "Is all of this why you want to move to Oklahoma?"

And here was the leverage this discussion could give him. Leo would use whatever info he could to keep her from taking Cameron out of state.

"It's part of it," she admitted.

But only part.

Leo wouldn't like to know that he was the main reason for her intended move.

He was obviously waiting for her to finish her explanation, but Olivia didn't get a chance to say anything else because his phone dinged. When he pulled it from his pocket, she saw Barrett's name on the screen.

"I need to take this call," Leo grumbled. "We'll finish our conversation when I'm done."

That last part sounded a little like a threat, and he hit the answer button while he went across the room and into the hall. No doubt so that he wouldn't wake Cameron. But Olivia followed him. This was likely an update about the investigation. Or more. It could be a warning that another attack was on the way. That possibility had her leaving the nursery door open in case she had to hurry in and scoop up the baby.

"Please give me good news," Leo said to his

brother, and he surprised her by putting the call on speaker. Olivia had thought Leo would want to process any bad news before passing it along to her.

"Sorry, but I don't have any," Barrett quickly answered. "I just got a preliminary report on Milton. He's been in and out of mental health facilities for years. I can't get access to his medical records, but I've arranged for him to have a psychiatric eval. Unfortunately, that won't happen until morning when the doctor from San Antonio can get here."

"The doctor might be able to convince you that Milton is a liar," Olivia insisted.

There was silence, both from Barrett and Leo. Barrett might not have known she was listening, so perhaps he was rethinking the conversation he'd intended to have with his brother.

"Leo, are you okay with Olivia being there?" Barrett came out and asked after several long moments.

Leo paused again, just a heartbeat this time, but Olivia already knew the answer. No, he wasn't *okay* staying under the same roof with her. That wouldn't improve once they finished the talk they'd started before this phone call.

"I want to keep Cameron and Olivia safe," Leo finally said. "I stand a better chance of doing that with them here."

This time Barrett's response wasn't silence but a slight sound that could have meant anything. However, Olivia was pretty sure it was the concern that he hadn't been able to tamp down. Barrett was no doubt worried she'd hurt his little brother all over again.

And she could.

No matter what she did, Leo could end up getting hurt. Or worse. She needed to do whatever it took to make sure *or worse* didn't happen.

"Since Olivia can hear this, I just got an interesting call from Rena Oldham," Barrett threw out there.

Olivia pulled back her shoulders. Rena was her dad's girlfriend. Or rather his on-again, off-again girlfriend. Rena had held that particular status for years. Their pattern was for them to be together for a couple of months, break up and see other people, only to start up their relationship again.

"What'd Rena want?" Olivia asked.

"Info about Samuel and you. Info I didn't give her," Barrett quickly added. "Apparently, she'd heard about the attack and said she was worried, that Samuel hadn't answered his phone when she'd tried to call him."

"My dad often doesn't take her calls. And Rena can be…clingy," she settled for saying.

"She can apparently also be opinionated, and she doesn't appear to have a high opinion of you. She wanted to know if you had anything to do with the attack tonight."

Olivia groaned. "Even if Rena thought I was capable of something like that, she knows that I'd never put my child in danger."

"I mentioned that to her," Barrett assured her, "and then I ended the call because I had better things to do. She did say, though, that she was out looking for your dad, so she might try to get onto Leo's ranch. Just a heads-up."

The ranch hands wouldn't allow that. Well, hopefully they wouldn't because Olivia didn't want to deal with Rena and her drama tonight.

"What about the second attacker? Any sign of him?" Leo asked.

"No, but Milton said that Olivia hired him and a couple of other attackers to go after you."

"She didn't."

Barrett made a sound, as if reserving judgment about that.

"She didn't," Leo repeated, sounding much more adamant this time.

That helped with the tightness in Olivia's chest. Having Leo believe her was a start because she was going to need him on her side. She had to convince him to do some things that would keep him safe.

"If Milton was right about someone hiring other thugs," Barrett went on, "then I need to find them so I can question them. Maybe then, we can figure out what the heck is going on. What's your theory as to who's behind this?"

"Randall is my top pick," Leo answered without hesitation.

"I figured you'd say that, and that's why I called him. Or rather, I tried to call him. He didn't answer his cell, so I called his house. His sister, Kristin, answered. She said Randall was staying overnight with a friend in San Antonio. She didn't have the friend's name or contact info."

Leo groaned softly and rubbed his free hand over his face. "Kristin would lie for him."

"Oh yeah," Barrett agreed.

Olivia was right there with his agreement. She didn't actually know Randall's sister, but from what she'd heard, the siblings were very close. And both bitter that Leo was trying to put Randall behind bars for murder.

"I'm also trying to find out if Randall actually sent that text to Olivia's father," Barrett went on. "My guess is that he didn't. Randall wouldn't be that stupid."

"No," Leo quietly answered, glancing back at the crib when Cameron stirred a little.

Olivia did the same and moved a little closer to the baby but not so close that she wouldn't be able to hear the rest of Leo and Barrett's conversation.

"But maybe Randall did it using a burner cell," Leo continued. "One that couldn't be traced back to him. Then, it'd be sort of a reverse psychology. His lawyers could argue that he's innocent because he wouldn't implicate himself."

It sickened Olivia to consider that Randall's hatred of Leo was at the core of the attacks. A man who hated that much wouldn't care if an innocent child got hurt during his quest for revenge.

"I'll see what I can learn about Randall's whereabouts," Barrett assured his brother. "In the meantime, try to get some rest. If you get any kind of signal that something's wrong, just call me. I'll be working from home."

That was good because Barrett lived only a couple of minutes from Leo. The ranch hands were decent backup, but if there was another attempt on their lives, she wanted Barrett there.

Leo ended the call and stared at the phone a moment as if to process his thoughts. When he turned toward her, Olivia knew what he wanted. And it didn't have anything to do with this heat zinging back and forth between them.

"Cut to the chase," Leo said, his voice low but with an edge. "Tell me about your father and this move you want to make to Oklahoma."

Olivia mentally tried to go through her answer and decided there was no way she could sugarcoat this. No way to stop Leo from doing something— maybe something bad—about this gut feeling she had.

She gathered her breath before she spoke. "First of all, I don't have any actual proof, but this isn't something I can keep to myself." Olivia had to pause again. "I believe my father could have been the one who hired Milton to kill you."

## Chapter Five

Olivia's words played through Leo's head for most of the night and had cost him some sleep. Of course, he probably wouldn't have actually gotten any sleep what with a would-be killer after him, but Olivia's accusation had only added more fuel to his mountain of worry. Not for himself but for Cameron.

And for Olivia, too, he reluctantly admitted.

Leo knew it had cost her to tell him about her fear that her father had possibly hired Milton. She'd always been protective of Samuel. Or so he'd thought. But in hindsight, he had to wonder if it was something else that'd kept her from straying too far from her father's side.

Fear.

That was something he'd pressed her about last night, but after dropping her bombshell, she'd dodged giving him any real answers to his questions and had insisted on going to bed. Her bottom line was that she didn't have any proof her father was guilty of hiring Milton or of killing her mother.

Only the feeling in the pit of her stomach that something wasn't right.

He believed in those kinds of feelings. As a cop, trusting his gut had even saved his butt a time or two. That's why Leo had already started digging into not only her mother's car accident but also looking for a money trail that would lead from Milton right back to Samuel.

Leo poured himself another cup of coffee, already his fourth of the morning, and it was barely 7:00 a.m. He doubted it'd be his last because he'd need the caffeine to keep him alert and focused. He used some of that focus now to go through the reports and the latest emails on the investigation.

He turned when he heard the footsteps and spotted Olivia making her way into the kitchen. The diaper bag looped over her shoulder, she was carrying a squirming Cameron. She looked harried, and Leo immediately figured out why. Cameron's clothes were a little askew and, along with those wiggles and squirms, he was making fussing sounds. No doubt because he hadn't wanted to be dressed. The boy preferred stripping down to his diaper.

"You should have come and gotten me when he woke up," Leo said, setting his coffee aside so he could take the baby. Despite all the bad stuff going on, he gave Cameron a smile and a kiss. "I would have helped."

"I didn't want to pull you away from your work."

Olivia's gaze drifted to his laptop open on the kitchen table. "Anything?"

He debated what to say and just went with the truth. "I've uncovered nothing that links your father to Milton. Not yet anyway." He would have continued, but Olivia interrupted him.

"How's your arm?" she asked.

Leo scowled when he glanced down at the bandage, one that an EMT had put on him after he'd cleaned the wound. It still throbbed, but he was hoping the over-the-counter pain meds would soon kick in and give him some relief.

"It's fine," he lied. "Are you ready to continue that discussion we started last night?"

However, the moment he asked it, he knew it'd have to wait a little longer. Cameron pointed to the high chair and kicked his legs to let Leo know he was ready for his breakfast. Olivia moved closer to help with that. As Leo strapped the baby into the chair, she took the makings for oatmeal from the diaper bag.

Olivia didn't look at Leo while she began to prepare the oatmeal, and she didn't object when he took the bag of cut-up fruit that he kept on hand for Cameron's visits. Leo put out some bits of peaches and pears that Cameron could manage to eat on his own. That kept him occupied while Leo turned to Olivia.

"*I believe my father could have been the one who hired Milton to kill you,*" Leo repeated to her to refresh her memory, though he was dead certain no refreshing was necessary.

She still didn't look at him, but Leo saw her hand tremble a little as she stirred the oatmeal. He finally took hold of her hand and turned her to face him. He saw it then. The fear. And he didn't think it was all related to the attack. It made Leo take a step back, but almost immediately Olivia stopped him by catching the sleeve of his shirt. It was the first time in ages that Leo remembered her actually touching him.

And he reacted.

Hell. His stupid body didn't seem to get it—that Olivia was off-limits. Not just because of the custody battle, either, but because it was obvious she was keeping things from him.

"Are you afraid of your father?" he came out and asked.

She opened her mouth, closed it and then squeezed her eyes shut a moment. "My father threatened you."

That was no big surprise. Samuel was always slinging barbs at him. But this seemed different. "Threatened me how?"

Olivia drew in a breath, moistened her lips. "He said if I stayed with you, that he'd figure out a way to ruin you. I was furious and told him to back off, but he said it'd be a shame if something happened to Cameron's father. Something that would take you out of the picture completely."

Okay, so her father had never actually made comments like that to Leo's face. With reason. Samuel probably hadn't wanted to risk arrest or to have Leo kick his butt. There was only so much he could take from the likes of Samuel Nash.

"You believed him?" Leo prodded.

He could tell the answer was yes even before Olivia nodded. And Leo didn't have any trouble filling in some very important blanks.

"Your father's threats are the reason you want to move to Oklahoma," he stated. It wasn't a question. "You want to put some distance between him and you."

She didn't nod. Didn't have to. He could see the confirmation in her eyes.

Leo felt the slam of anger that Samuel would try to manipulate Olivia this way. "Why the heck didn't you tell me?" But again, he knew the answer. "You knew I'd confront him."

"Yes," she admitted. "And I figured one of two things would happen. He'd hurt you, or you'd hurt him. Or kill him," Olivia added in a mumble. "That would have likely sent you to jail."

"Maybe, but it would have been worth it." Of course, that was the anger talking. Leo didn't want to go to jail and be separated from his son. Especially if Samuel would still be around to bully and threaten Olivia so he could try to bend her to his will. And that made him wonder something else.

Just how long had this bullying been going on?

Since it wouldn't necessarily be easy for her to answer, Leo checked on Cameron first. The boy was still chowing down on the fruit, but Leo added more to the tray to keep him occupied a couple of minutes longer.

He then turned back to Olivia. Leo had geared up to verbally blast her for not telling him all of this sooner, but she hadn't shut down her feelings fast enough. And he saw it.

The toll this had taken on her.

He wasn't immune to the emotion on her face. Leo didn't know everything about what she'd been through, but obviously it'd been plenty.

Before he could think, or stop himself, he reached out to pull her into his arms. He assured himself it was something he would do for plenty of people. But Olivia wasn't just anybody. She had been his lover, and this kind of contact was at best ill-advised and at worst, just plain stupid.

She made a small sound, a moan that sounded as if it was from both relief and pleasure. It confirmed the "just plain stupid" part. No way should they be playing with fire like this. Of course, if they gave in to the heat, it would fix some things. At least it would get them on the same side again.

Olivia didn't stay in his arms, though. She pulled back, moving several inches away, and he could practically feel her putting up barriers between them. "It was my decision," she blurted out.

Leo considered that a moment and bit off saying

the profanity that nearly made its way to his mouth. "Exactly what decision are you talking about?" He was pretty sure he knew, but he wanted to hear it. And when he did, he figured he'd be doing plenty more mental cursing.

Olivia swallowed hard, but he had to hand it to her. She steeled herself, squaring her shoulders and looking him straight in the eyes. "To end things with you. If I hadn't," she quickly added in a whisper, "my father would have made our lives a living hell."

This time, the slam of anger was stronger. A hot smash of heat that hit him in the gut and spread. "You broke up with me to keep things smooth with Samuel." He'd had to speak through clenched teeth.

She didn't break eye contact with him. "Our relationship had run its course. I didn't see any reason to keep hanging on to it when it could have caused both of us so much trouble."

*Our relationship had run its course.* Well, that was news to him, but it explained why she'd given in to her father. If she'd loved Leo—hell, if she'd just cared enough about him—she would have stood with him so they could handle the *trouble* together.

"Besides," she went on a moment later, "this made things more peaceful for Cameron. I didn't want him to be around all the negativity."

He gave her a flat look to remind her that there was plenty of negativity over their custody fight and her plans to move to Oklahoma. He would have told her that verbally if Cameron hadn't started to fuss. Both Olivia and he turned toward the boy, but before Leo could go to him, his phone rang.

"It's Barrett," he relayed to Olivia after glancing at the screen. It was a call he had to take.

Leo went to the other side of the room, taking up position by the sink so he could keep watch out the back window. Olivia got started feeding Cameron his oatmeal, but Leo had no doubt she'd want to hear what his brother had to say. That's why he put the call on speaker.

"Olivia's listening," Leo told Barrett right off. "She and Cameron are in the kitchen with me." That would cue his brother to tone down whatever he had to say. "Is everything okay?"

"I was going to ask you that," Barrett countered. "Things are fine here. No signs of any other attackers."

"Same here. You got my email about Samuel? I'm running a financial check on your father," Leo added to Olivia when she looked at him.

"I got it, and I'll help you with that when I clear up some things."

"One of those things is Milton," Leo supplied.

Barrett made a sound of agreement. "The psychiatrist will be here any minute. I'll let you know as soon as she's done with her eval. In the meantime, I managed to get access to sealed juvie records for Milton."

It didn't surprise Leo that there was a juvie re-

cord since Milton had also been arrested as an adult for larceny, assault and public intoxication. He'd had no cage time though, only parole.

"Milton's pretty much been in trouble since he was old enough to sneak out of his house at night," Barrett continued. "And he has a history of violence. I'll send you the records to read for yourself, but Milton has a bad habit of being an accessory, situations where he was talked into doing something illegal or just plain stupid."

Leo would indeed read the reports, but he trusted Barrett's interpretation. It meant that Milton had possibly been coerced this time. Hell. More than possibly. Highly likely. Because, as Olivia had pointed out, her father could be behind this. Except that left Leo with one Texas-sized inconsistency. Even with all his faults, Samuel wouldn't have endangered Cameron.

"I'll need Olivia's official statement on the attack," Barrett went on. "And you can't be the one to take it."

No, because there were already enough conflicts of interest without adding that to the mix. "I'm keeping Cameron and Olivia in protective custody," Leo stated, though he was certain his brother already knew that.

"I've got no problem with that, but it means you'll either have to bring her here or else I'll need to go out to your place. I'm short-handed right now, but I should be able to get there by early afternoon."

Leo knew his brother was in a bind when it came to manpower, especially since Leo himself wouldn't be able to do his regular shift, but he wouldn't take Olivia outside unless he was certain it was safe.

"I'll let you know," he told Barrett. "Call me if you get any updates."

He'd just ended the call when he heard the sound of a car engine. Every muscle in his body went on alert, and in the same moment, a text flashed on his screen. It was from Wally.

Cameron's nanny just arrived, Wally had texted. Is it okay to let her in?

"What's wrong?" Olivia immediately asked. "Who's here?"

"Izzie," Leo quickly assured her, some of his own tension easing because Wally would have recognized the nanny on site. So, this wasn't a situation of someone trying to sneak onto the ranch.

Olivia released a breath that she'd obviously been holding. "I called Izzie last night and told her what was going on. I'm sorry I forgot to tell you that she'd insisted on coming in case we needed help."

Leo thought they might indeed need help with the baby, but he didn't like that Izzie was out and about and could therefore get caught up in another attack.

"Wait here," he told Olivia. "And stay away from the windows."

That last part was something he should have already warned Olivia about, but he'd let their

conversation—and her—distract him. Not good. Right now a distraction could be fatal.

Leo went to the front of the house and disengaged the security system only long enough to open the front door and motion for the nanny to hurry inside. Izzie did. She raced across the yard and onto the porch.

As usual, the woman was wearing jeans and a plain cotton shirt, and she had her hair scooped up in a ponytail. Leo had run a background check on the nanny when Olivia had first hired her, and he knew Izzie was forty-nine and had a twenty-three-year-old son. She'd been a nanny for the past fifteen years. Plenty of experience and no smudges.

"Are all of you okay?" she immediately asked.

Izzie looked exactly as he'd expected. Worried. *Welcome to the club.*

"We're okay for now. I want to keep it that way." He shut the door, locked it and rearmed the security system. Leo also glanced out the front windows to make sure no one had followed Izzie. He didn't see anyone and was certain that if Wally spotted an intruder, he'd call ASAP.

"Olivia and Cameron are in the kitchen," Leo told the woman.

He motioned for her to follow him even though Izzie knew the layout of his house. She'd been there several times since Olivia had had the nanny drop off Cameron for his visits when Olivia hadn't been able to do it herself.

Izzie greeted Olivia with a hug and murmured some reassurances that all would be well before she went to Cameron to greet him. Leo reached for his laptop, intending to take it into the living room so he could read Milton's juvie records, but he stopped when his phone rang again. He didn't recognize the number on the screen, and he got an immediate jolt of concern. It was too early for a telemarketer, but this could be connected to the investigation. Sometimes, would-be killers liked to taunt and gloat.

"Deputy Logan," he answered, ready to hit the record function on his phone. But it wasn't a stranger's voice he heard.

"It's me, Bernice Saylor," the caller said.

Since Bernice made a habit of giving him the cold shoulder whenever he ran into her, he couldn't imagine why she'd want to talk to him. Then he remembered that Olivia didn't have her phone and Bernice might not know the number of her prepaid cell.

"I'm sorry for calling at such an early hour," Bernice said.

"Did you want to speak to Olivia?" he asked.

"No. I need to talk to you. It's important. It's about the attack."

That got his attention. "What about it?"

"I need to talk to you in person," Bernice insisted. "I have information you need to hear. I believe I know who's trying to kill you."

## Chapter Six

Olivia wasn't certain what Bernice had just told Leo, but whatever it was, he abruptly stepped out of the kitchen and motioned for her to join him. Olivia did, handing off the oatmeal to Izzie so that the nanny could finish feeding Cameron.

"Bernice, I need you to repeat what you just said," Leo instructed.

Even though he didn't put the call on speaker, Olivia moved close enough so she could listen. She figured this would be some kind of ploy to get her to mend fences with her father. Bernice was not objective when it came to Samuel. In fact, Olivia believed the woman was in love with him. Not that her father would return that love. No. Her dad relied on Bernice, but the woman fell very much into the close employee category.

"I told you that I believe I know who's trying to kill you," Bernice said.

Everything inside Olivia went still. She'd never known Bernice to say a negative thing about her father, but maybe the woman had seen or heard something to change her mind.

"Who?" Olivia blurted. "My father?"

She had no idea if Leo wanted her to make her presence known, but Olivia wanted to hear every word of this conversation. That included Bernice's answer to her question.

Bernice made a sharp sound of surprise. "No, not your father. Of course not him. Samuel would never do anything like that."

As far as Olivia was concerned, that was to be determined. Leo apparently felt the same way. "You're sure about that?" he fired back at Bernice.

"Positive. Samuel is a good man who loves his daughter and grandson. He wouldn't hurt you because it'd hurt them."

Again, that was to be determined. "Then who tried to kill Leo?" Olivia prompted, not waiting for the woman to respond before she added, "And you'd better not accuse me of it."

There was a long moment of silence before Bernice spoke. "Not you. But Samuel told me what happened with someone using your phone, and I think I know who's responsible. Rena Oldham."

"Samuel's girlfriend," Leo supplied.

"Ex-girlfriend," Bernice corrected. "Samuel broke things off with her a few days ago. She was pressuring him for marriage, again, and he got fed up with it."

Olivia didn't bother asking Bernice how she became privy to such private information because it was possible she'd learned it from the source— Samuel. If not, Bernice would have made it her business to find out what'd happened. Olivia suspected there was very little that went on at the family estate that Bernice didn't know about.

Well, very little except for the real reason that Olivia had planned to move to Oklahoma. Bernice hadn't seemed to latch onto the fact that Olivia had been planning to protect Leo.

For all the good it'd done.

It certainly hadn't stopped someone from trying to kill him.

"Are you saying that you think Rena Oldham conspired to commit murder?" Leo bluntly challenged.

More silence. "Yes," Bernice finally answered. "And I have some things I think will convince you to arrest her."

"What things?" Leo snapped.

"I'm not getting into this over the phone. I'll meet you at the sheriff's office, but I want you to bring in Rena, too. I want you to question her after you see what I have."

Leo groaned. "You can take whatever you think you've got to my brother, Sheriff Barrett Logan. I'll call him to let him know to expect you."

"No." Bernice definitely didn't pause this time. "I'll only talk to you, so if you want to see what I have, you'll meet me at the sheriff's office. I'm sure Olivia will be very interested in what I have, too."

Olivia was close enough to Leo to see his eyes go cop flat. "If you're withholding evidence pertinent to an investigation, that's a crime. A felony. You want to be arrested Bernice?"

"No." Again, no pause, and there was a bitter edge to her voice. "If you won't meet me at the sheriff's office, then come here to Samuel's estate, or I can go to your place."

"You're not coming here," he snapped but then paused when he got an incoming call.

Olivia saw that it was from Barrett.

"I'll have to call you back," Leo told Bernice. Without waiting for her response, he switched over to his brother's call. "Is something wrong?" he asked Barrett.

"I'm not sure."

And just those three words put Olivia on full alert. Leo, too, and they both turned toward the kitchen to make sure Cameron was okay. He was. Izzie had moved him away from the window and was feeding him the rest of his breakfast. Thankfully, their son was oblivious to any bad news they were about to hear.

"Milton's psychiatrist isn't here yet, but he's insisting on talking to Olivia," Barrett explained. "In fact, he says he'll make a full confession to her."

"A confession," Leo repeated, and she heard the skepticism in Leo's tone. "Has he made any calls, ones where he could have arranged another attack?"

"No. But I think he's coming down from whatever high he was on. He's been pacing his cell and mumbling about this all being a mistake. I pressed him on exactly what mistake he meant, but he insisted he'd only talk to Olivia."

"It could still be a trap," Leo muttered moments later.

"Could be," Barrett agreed. "But if so, he would have had to set up an attack before his arrest. He was allowed one call, and he didn't use it, not even to contact a lawyer."

Interesting, but that didn't mean the man didn't have something up his sleeve. Still, Olivia would like to hear what Milton had to say.

"I wouldn't want to take Cameron to the sheriff's office," Olivia insisted. "But if you could arrange for a deputy to be here with him, maybe Leo and I can come in. My father's household manager, Bernice Saylor, wants Leo to meet her there, so we could kill two birds with one stone."

"Why does the household manager want to meet you?" Barrett immediately asked.

It was Leo who answered. "She claims that Samuel's ex-girlfriend is the person responsible for the attack and says she has proof. In fact, Bernice wants the ex brought in for questioning, which might not be a bad idea. Her name is Rena Oldham."

"She's Samuel's ex, you said?" Barrett questioned.

"According to Bernice, she is," Olivia explained. "She's been my father's longtime girlfriend, and they've broken up before. I didn't know about this particular breakup, though."

Barrett stayed silent a few long moments, obviously processing that. "You think Rena's capable of setting up a murder?"

Olivia hadn't had much time to consider the possibility, but she gave it some thought now. "Maybe. She's been on and off with my father for years, and she has a temper. She also claims she's in love with him, so I'm not sure how she'd react if he truly did end things with her for good."

"I'll bring her in for questioning," Barrett assured them. "Where does she live?"

"Culver Crossing." That wasn't far at all and was in the same town where Olivia lived. If Barrett could get in touch with Rena, he might have the woman in his office in under a half hour.

"What about Bernice?" Barrett asked. "Want me to bring her in, as well?"

"Sure. But I can text her," Leo said. "Can you spare a deputy to be with Cameron and his nanny?"

"I'll do better than that. I'm texting Daniel as we speak. He can be at your place in just a few minutes, and he can stay with Izzie and the baby."

Olivia released the breath she'd been holding. Along with being a deputy, Daniel was Leo's brother. He'd do everything within his power to protect Cameron.

"Keep your ranch hands on alert," Barrett advised. "And I'm sending Scottie out to your place for backup. He'll arrive in the cruiser, and Olivia and you can ride with him to town. He won't be able to stay once he's dropped you off because he's not on duty, but I'll get you back home after we're done here."

Again, Olivia was relieved. Scottie Bronson was yet another deputy, one that she knew Leo trusted. Plus, a police cruiser would be a lot safer than a regular vehicle. Still, it would mean leaving Cameron, and Olivia knew that wouldn't be easy, not even for a short time. But if they could get answers to help the investigation, it would ultimately make things safer for her little boy.

"I say we go ahead and bring in Randall," Barrett added. "And Samuel. That way I can ask about alibis and maybe rile at least one of them enough to spill something."

Her father would indeed be riled at being treated as a suspect, but Barrett was right. Sometimes, pushing the right buttons led to answers, and they very much needed answers right now.

Leo ended the call with his brother and immediately texted Bernice to let her know they would meet her at the sheriff's office. Bernice responded with I'm already on the way there.

Good. Olivia didn't exactly relish the idea of dealing with Bernice, but at least this way they wouldn't have to wait long for her to arrive. Besides, if Bernice actually had proof about Rena being involved in this, then maybe Barrett would be able to make an arrest today.

Olivia went back in the kitchen to tell Izzie their plans and to finish feeding Cameron, but only a couple of minutes had passed before she heard the sound of a car engine. Leo's phone also dinged with a text.

"It's Daniel," he relayed. "He's here." And he headed to the door to let his brother in.

Olivia filled in Izzie while Leo and Daniel made their way to the kitchen. Daniel's eyes met hers, and she felt the chill. No doubt because Daniel didn't care much for the custody fight she was giving Leo.

Correction—the fight she *had given* Leo.

Once the danger had passed, she really did need to figure out what to do. If her father was behind the attacks, then her leaving could end up only making things worse.

"Olivia," Daniel greeted, his voice as cool as his eyes. Ironic since they were a genetic copy of Leo's and Cameron's. Thankfully, though, there was no chill when Daniel went to Cameron and brushed a kiss on the top of his head.

Cameron babbled a greeting, grinned and offered Daniel a piece of peach. Obviously, her son was very comfortable around Leo's brother.

"I didn't see anything unusual on the drive over," Daniel explained. "But keep watch. I'll do the same."

Leo nodded in thanks. "I'll text Wally and explain to him what's happening." He shifted his attention to Izzie. "Daniel and some of my hands will be on guard while Olivia and I are out."

"We won't be gone long," Olivia assured the woman. She hoped that was true.

She could tell that Izzie was trying to put on a brave face. Olivia was doing the same thing, and she tried to keep up the pretense that this was just a normal breakfast while they waited for Scottie. However, the moment Leo got the text that the deputy was in front of the house, her nerves and fears returned. Not fear for herself but for Cameron.

"He'll be fine," Daniel said as if reading her mind. He ruffled Cameron's hair, grinned at him.

Olivia wanted to rattle off some instructions, repeating for them to stay away from the windows and reminding them to lock the doors. But Daniel would know to do those things. Once Scottie arrived, Olivia had to force herself out of the kitchen, but she didn't do that until she'd given Cameron several kisses.

When Leo led her out the front door, she saw that Scottie had parked the cruiser directly in front of the house. She also spotted the ranch hands that were standing guard.

As soon as Leo and she were in the back seat, Scottie took off. He didn't offer any greetings, instead keeping his attention on their surroundings. Leo and she did the same. She doubted a gunman would come after them in broad daylight, but she couldn't be sure since she didn't know who or what they were dealing with.

Soon, she hoped, that would change.

"I'm sorry," she muttered to Leo.

His gaze practically snapped toward her. He didn't ask "what for," but she could see the question in his eyes.

"I'm sorry for…everything," she settled for saying. "But especially for not telling you sooner about my father."

A muscle flickered in his jaw before he made a sound of agreement. Maybe he was accepting her apology, or it could be this was simply a discussion he didn't want to have in front of Scottie. Either way, it was her signal to table the subject. That was probably a good thing. It was best to have everything worked out in her mind before she had to hash things out with Leo.

Leo's phone rang, and he snatched it from his jeans' pocket. It was an understatement that they were both on edge, and Olivia immediately began to consider all the worst-cast scenarios.

"It's Randall," he told her.

That certainly didn't make her relax. After all, it was possible that Randall had been the one to hire Milton.

Leo hit the answer button and, like before, Olivia was close enough to hear when Randall snarled, "Deputy Logan, are you trying to get your butt sued?" The man didn't wait for an answer. "Because you and your sheriff brother are harassing me by dragging me in for an interrogation this morning, and that's grounds for a lawsuit."

"The sheriff and I want you in for questioning," Leo stated. "You have means, motive and opportunity for attempted murder of a law enforcement officer. Me," Leo clarified just in case Randall had any doubts.

"I have an alibi," Randall wailed. "My sister told you where I was when you got knifed. I wasn't anywhere near Mercy Ridge or you."

Leo fired right back. "You know that doesn't get you off the hook. Someone hired the idiot who came after me, and you're a person of interest."

Randall spewed a string of raw profanity. "You're just pissed off because you couldn't pin murder on me, and you can't pin this one on me, either." He did more cursing. "I'll bring my lawyer for this witch hunt of an interrogation. Then I'll be filing that lawsuit right after. You'd better be prepared to pony up lots of cash because I'll sue you for every penny the Logans have." With that, Randall ended the call.

If Leo was concerned about the threat of a possible lawsuit, he didn't show it. He just dragged in a weary breath and continued to keep watch.

It took Scottie less than fifteen minutes to reach the sheriff's office, but every mile felt like an eternity to Olivia. So did the mere seconds it took to get out of the cruiser and inside. She immediately tried to steel herself up for Bernice, but the woman wasn't there. There was only a female deputy at the dispatch/reception desk and Barrett, who was making his way from his office toward them.

"The psychiatrist has been delayed, Bernice and Rena should be here any minute," Barrett told them. "Randall is due in an hour, and Samuel will be in this afternoon."

"Randall called me a couple of minutes ago," Leo informed him. "He wanted to express his disapproval at being called in." He dragged his hand over his face. "This smacks of something Randall could have done, and he's at the top of my suspect list."

"Mine, too," Barrett agreed. "What better way to get back at you than to have you murdered and to set up the mother of your child to take the blame?"

That put a huge knot in Olivia's stomach. Because it could be true. All of this could be about revenge, and Randall probably wouldn't care if Cameron became collateral damage.

"I'll go ahead and move Milton to an interview room so he can get started with that confession he says he wants to give you," Barrett added to Olivia. "Leo and I will be in there with you, and I'll also be recording everything that's said."

She nodded and had fully expected the recording. What Olivia hadn't expected was to be in the same room with Milton. She had thought she'd be speaking to him while he was behind bars. In hindsight, she should have realized that Barrett would need to make this an official interrogation.

"Wait here, and I'll get Milton," Barrett said, heading in the direction of where Olivia figured the holding cells were.

"Want some coffee?" Leo asked, going to the small serving area on the far side of the room.

However, he stopped when a bell rang to indicate the front door had just opened. The adrenaline shot through her when she saw Leo place his hand over his weapon, and she whirled around to see what had caused that reaction.

Rena Oldham walked in.

She wasn't what anyone would call willowy. In fact, she had what Olivia thought of as an Amazon warrior's build on a sturdy five-foot, ten-inch frame. Rena obviously worked out a lot, too, because her arms and legs were well toned.

Despite the somewhat early hour, the woman looked well put together in her red summer pants, white top and sandals. There wasn't a strand of her shoulder-length honey-blond hair out of place. Ditto for her perfectly applied makeup, but then again Olivia had never seen her look any other way. Bernice had mentioned something about Rena being in her fifties, but she looked much younger than that.

"Where's Bernice?" Rena snarled, and her tone gave Olivia a taste of the temper that she'd mentioned to Leo. "I want to confront that busybody witch for lying about me."

Leo skipped getting any coffee and went to Olivia's side. "How'd you know Bernice is lying?"

"Because she called me and told me she was coming here, and that she had so-called proof that I'm the one responsible for you and Olivia nearly being killed." Rena turned her cool blue eyes on Olivia then. "I didn't have anything to do with that."

"So, why does Bernice think you did?" Leo challenged.

"Because she's a jealous, vindictive witch," Rena readily supplied. "She doesn't want anyone near her precious Samuel except her. Well, she can have him. I'm done with Samuel."

So, it was true that her father and Rena had broken up. Not really a surprise. Olivia had been down this path with them before.

"What exactly does Bernice have that she's calling proof of your guilt?" Leo asked.

Rena threw her hands in the air. "Your guess is as good as mine. But whatever it is, it doesn't point to me as a would-be killer because I'm not one. You put that on whatever official record you need."

Leo nodded. "Let's move this conversation to an interview room." He motioned for them to follow him, but they hadn't even reached the hall when Barrett came out with Milton.

Everyone froze.

Milton's gaze zoomed right to Olivia, and he smiled. She felt the flash of disgust followed by the rage. This SOB had tried to kill Leo and had tried to pin that on her. Olivia glared at him and had to rein in that rage to keep from going to him and slapping him. But Milton's attention was no longer on her. He looked at Rena.

And smiled again.

This was a different kind of smile, though. Not a taunt like the one he'd doled out to her. This one had a glimmer of recognition, and his eyes practically lit up. Rena, however, didn't have that reaction. She squared her shoulders and groaned softly.

"You two know each other?" Leo asked, clearly picking up on their body language.

"No," Rena said at the same moment that Milton answered. "Yeah, we do."

Leo aimed a scowl at Rena. "Do you know this man?" he pressed.

Rena huffed. "He knew my brother, Brett. They were drug users, so I distanced myself from both of them."

"Then, you do know Milton," Leo stated, his voice flat. Obviously, he didn't care for the lie that Rena had told with her previous response.

Annoyance and anger sparked through Rena's eyes. "If you're trying to connect me to this piece of scum, then you'd better stop right there. I haven't seen or spoken to Milton in years, not since my brother died of an overdose from drugs that this snake gave him." She tipped her head at Milton to indicate *he* was that *snake*.

Milton tried to shrug despite the fact that he was cuffed and Barrett had his arm in a grip. "Brett supplied me with plenty of stuff, too. I just got lucky and he didn't."

Rena took a step toward him as if she might launch herself at him. Since Olivia had wanted to do the same thing just minutes earlier, she totally understood the woman's reaction. But Leo stepped in front of Rena to stop her. No way did he want a brawl when they hadn't even had a chance to deal with Milton.

"Wait here," Leo ordered Rena, and he glanced at the deputy at the desk. According to her name tag, she was Cybil Cassidy. "Stay with Miss Oldham while Olivia and I have a chat with Milton."

"I've changed my mind," Milton blurted when they started for the interview room. He smiled at Olivia again. "I've decided I don't want to make a confession, after all."

Olivia muttered some profanity before she could stop herself, and she got a second slam of anger. "Why not?" she demanded.

With a ghost of that sly smile still on his mouth, he shook his head. "I'm not feeling well. I should probably talk to the psychiatrist first. Then, if I'm feeling better, you and I can have a heart to heart."

Coming from Milton, that last part sounded like a threat. Felt like one, too.

"What kind of sick game are you playing?" Leo demanded, going closer to Milton.

Milton looked Leo straight in the eye. "I'm a sick man, didn't you know? And it's my right not to say anything that could incriminate me."

"Was this a ploy to get us off the ranch so some-one else can try to kill us?" Olivia quickly asked.

Leo had already gone there, and he fired off a text to Daniel to make sure everything was okay. Daniel gave him an equally quick response to let him know that it was. Leo then warned his brother to be extra cautious, though he figured Daniel was already doing just that.

Leo shifted his attention back to Milton and didn't break the intense stare he had with the man until the door opened again. This time there were two visitors, both women. The first to walk in was a tall, slim woman with auburn hair that fell right at her chin. Leo didn't know her, but he figured she was the psychia-trist. Leo had no trouble recognizing the second one.

Bernice.

Like Rena, she was tall, but that's where the similarities ended. Bernice had a stocky build with wide shoulders, and her dark brown hair was threaded with gray. No makeup, and her clothes didn't look as if they'd have a designer label. She wore a fitted gray dress that wouldn't have looked out of place on a hotel maid.

Bernice and Rena started a glaring match of their own, but Barrett handed off Milton to Deputy Cassidy with instructions to take him to the interview room.

"Dr. Kirkpatrick?" Barrett asked, and the woman nodded. Once he'd checked her ID, he motioned for her to follow Deputy Cassidy and Milton. "I want a copy of your eval as soon as you have it."

"I'll give you any information that I can," the doctor countered.

That meant she likely wouldn't tell Barrett everything that went on in the eval. She followed Milton and the deputy, leaving Olivia with Barrett, Leo, Rena and Bernice. The air was practically crackling with tension, and most of it was coming from Rena.

"How dare you accuse me of trying to kill someone," Rena said through clenched teeth. "You're vindictive and jealous, and you have nothing connecting me to any of this mess."

Bernice's glare softened when she turned to Leo. She took a large manila envelope from her purse and handed it to him.

"I think once you read everything in there, you'll see what I mean about Rena being the one who hired Milton," Bernice calmly stated.

"I didn't hire him," Rena practically shouted, and she tried to snatch the envelope from Leo. He shot her a look that could have frozen the deepest level of hell.

"What's in here?" Leo asked Bernice.

The woman took a deep breath before she answered. "Copies of emails that Rena sent Samuel after he broke up with her this last time. She threatened to get back at him."

Rena rolled her eyes, obviously dismissing that, but the anger stayed on her face. "I was furious and hurt. Those emails meant nothing. And you had no right to read them," she added to Bernice. "Those were private emails I sent to Samuel."

"I run the estate," Bernice pointed out. "That includes going through correspondence and emails. You threatened to get back at Samuel, and you said it'd be awful if something bad happened to someone he loved."

"I was angry," Rena argued. "I didn't mean it. I didn't mean it," she repeated, aiming her plea at Olivia.

Olivia had no idea if Rena had meant it or not. Maybe her temper had just gotten the best of her. Maybe not. She could be looking into the face of the person who'd set up the attack.

"Rena broke into the estate just yesterday," Bernice added. "I found her trying to go through Samuel's office when he wasn't there."

"I didn't break in." Rena's voice held as much of a snarl as Bernice's. "Samuel gave me a key and the security codes—"

Bernice just talked right over Rena. "I had the locks and security system changed last night after I insisted she leave the premises. She wouldn't tell me what she was looking for in Samuel's office, but I suspect she was there to steal something."

Rena gave the woman a much cooler look, her mouth curved into a sly smile. "I was looking for my earring that fell off when Samuel and I had sex on his desk. Did you listen in on that, too, Bernice? Did you get an eyeful of your *employer* getting down and dirty with me?"

Olivia groaned. That was so not an image she wanted in her head. Apparently, neither did Bernice because she gave Rena a cold stare.

"Samuel's with so many women that I don't notice such things," Bernice said, her voice as icy as the look. "You are one of dozens. *Dozens*," she stressed. "And none of them, including you, lasted."

That clearly rattled Rena. She opened her mouth, closed it and then narrowed her eyes. "Samuel still has feelings for me," Rena insisted. "You just wait and see. He'll come back to me. He always does."

"Keep thinking that," Bernice grumbled and turned to Leo. "I hired a PI to do a thorough background check on Rena, and I learned that she has criminal contacts. Your suspect, Milton Hough, for one. She knows him."

"So I just found out." Leo lifted the envelope and ignored the sound of outrage that Rena made. "I'll read what's in here, but I want to know if any of the emails mentioned Milton?"

"No. But there is something you might find interesting." Bernice tipped her head to the envelope. "Read the PI's report, and you'll see that Rena has another connection to you. Or rather, a connection to someone who wants you dead." She gave a satisfied nod. "Rena's been bedmates with none other than the man who'd do anything to ruin you."

"And who would that be?" Leo asked.

Bernice lifted her chin. "Randall Arnett."

## Chapter Seven

Randall Arnett.

Leo wasn't surprised to hear that particular name come up in this investigation, but he hadn't expected this kind of connection. He stared at Rena, waiting for an explanation. Olivia and Barrett were doing the same thing. However, it seemed to take Rena a couple of long moments just to compose herself.

Rena made a throaty sound and whipped out her phone. "I'm calling my lawyer."

"Good," Barrett advised her. "Because you're going to need one." He glanced at Leo. "You want to take her in for questioning, or should I do it?"

Leo stared at the envelope a moment. "I want to go through this envelope first. That'll give her lawyer a chance to get here."

Rena was already speaking to someone on the phone, presumably her attorney, and it made Leo wonder just how often the woman required legal services that she would be able to make contact this quickly. But that was a question for another time, another place. For now, he wanted to get a look at what Bernice had put in the envelope.

"You can have a seat out here," Barrett told Bernice. "I'll need to take your statement, too, but you'll have to wait your turn."

"Oh, I'll wait," Bernice assured him. "I'll do whatever it takes to get that piece of temperamental fluff out of Samuel's life."

Beside him, Leo saw Olivia go a little stiff. "You do this sort of thing often for my father?" she asked.

Bernice's chin came up. "I take care of him. Which is more than you do," she snapped. "He's worried sick about Cameron and you."

There it was again. The territorial attitude that Bernice had always had for Samuel. Normally, Leo didn't see anything especially sinister about it, but this felt…well, different.

Bernice had obviously gone to some expense and trouble to dig up dirt on Rena, but he knew from experience that a person doing the digging could be selective about what they found. In other words, Bernice could have looked solely for info to discredit a woman she saw as competition for Samuel's attention. Or a woman Bernice wanted to punish because she had not gone quietly after this latest breakup with Samuel.

Since he wanted to get Olivia away from Bernice—and away from the windows—he motioned for her to follow him. He didn't have an office of his own, none of the deputies did, so they went into Barrett's and he shut the door. He'd still be able to hear if anyone came in because the bell on the door would alert him, but this way he and Olivia would have some privacy to go through the envelope. Plus, there was no worry about Bernice not staying put. It was crystal-clear that the woman intended to put the screws to Rena.

Leo took a moment once they were alone to try to absorb all the information he'd just gotten from Rena and Bernice. Apparently, Olivia was doing the same because she didn't say anything, and he heard her draw in a long, deep breath and then slowly expel it.

"If there's anything in the emails, can you actually use it to arrest Rena?" she finally asked as she sank into the chair next to the desk.

Leo shrugged and sat, too. Opening the envelope, he took out the papers. "Maybe. There could be a chain of custody issue, though. Bernice could have altered the emails she's printed out, so we'd have to see the originals and verify that Rena did, indeed, send them."

Of course, Rena hadn't denied the sending part, only the intent. And intent in an email was hard to prove. Even if she'd threatened Samuel to hell and back, it didn't mean the woman had actually gone through on the threats. Then again, she did have those criminal contacts.

Including Randall.

Leo pondered that a moment while he glanced through the first email. Yeah, it was a threat, all right. One peppered with a lot of profanity, capital letters and exclamation marks. What he didn't see were any details of how Rena would carry through with getting back at her lover for dumping her. There were no specifics, no time and place references, just the "something awful" that might happen to someone Samuel loved.

But it wasn't as black and white as Bernice had painted it.

I was in love with you, Rena had written. Just imagine something awful happening to someone you love, and that's how I feel right now. You've crushed my heart, Samuel, and I hope that one day you'll hurt as much as I'm hurting now.

Definitely no "I'm going to kill someone you love" as Bernice had made it seem. Still, there was a lot of emotion in that handful of sentences, and sometimes emotion could cause people to do all sorts of bad things.

He handed the email to Olivia so she could read it for herself and then went onto the next one. There were five total, all where Rena had vented and spewed some venom. He passed those to Olivia, as well, and studied the next page. It was an account of what Bernice had overheard when Rena and Samuel had argued about the breakup. It was clearly hearsay, but if Samuel verified it, then it could be used to show that Rena had had motive to set up the attack.

"Did your father say anything to you about his breakup with Rena?" Leo asked Olivia.

"Nothing specific, but they've broken up so many

times that it's not something he'd talk to me about."
She looked up from the paper and their gazes met.
"It doesn't feel as if Rena would try to get back
at my father through you. With her hot temper, it
seems as if she'd just go directly after him."

"That'd be what everyone would expect. But
maybe Rena reined in her temper long enough to
figure that out. After all, if someone tried to kill
Samuel, she'd be a prime suspect. This way, he's still
punished because you were set up to take the blame
for the attack."

She nodded, took another of those long breaths.
"So, Rena could have hired her late brother's
friend." Olivia paused. "Or hired Randall."

"Yeah," Leo agreed as he put aside the rest of
Bernice's account of the breakup so he could look
through the PI's report.

It was thorough. That was Leo's first impression.
The PI had basically provided details of the last twenty
years of Rena's life. He'd used social media posts and
info that he'd garnered from her friends to detail a pattern of being with Samuel, followed by a breakup, followed by short romantic relationships with other men.
Short career ventures, too. Rena came from money
and had a trust fund, one that she'd practically drained
to set up one failed business after the other.

"If this report is accurate," Leo remarked to
Olivia, "then Rena is hurting financially. In fact,
she's flat broke and financing her lifestyle off credit

cards. Maybe that's one of the reasons she was pressing your father for marriage."

"Maybe," Olivia agreed. "But if she's broke, then she wouldn't have been able to pay Milton for the attack."

"No, but it could be she didn't need cash for that. Perhaps she just stirred him up enough. Or he could have done this as a favor since he knew her brother."

"Maybe," Olivia repeated, not sounding convinced.

Leo was on the same page with her. He wasn't convinced, either.

Olivia stood so she could read the report from over his shoulder. Of course, that meant her face ended up very close to his.

He caught her scent.

When she'd showered that morning, she'd obviously used the same brand of soap that he had. That's what would have been in the guest bath. It was pretty basic soap, but it managed to smell damn special on her since it mingled with her own unique scent. One that he remembered all too well. And one that stirred him in the wrong places.

"Rena was with Randall for about two and a half months," Olivia said, going through the report. She was totally unaware of the effect she was having on him. "Do I have the timing right? Rena was with Randall shortly after he was with the girlfriend who went missing?"

"Jessa McCade," Leo provided. Yes, the timing

was right for that. "I'll want to question Rena to find out if Randall said anything to her about Jessa. Or if Randall was ever violent with her—as I suspect he had been with Jessa."

In fact, Leo figured the violence had maybe started as an argument and had escalated when Randall had killed Jessa in a fit of temper. Then Randall had disposed of the body and it hadn't been found. It was the only thing that made sense to Leo since he wasn't buying that Jessa had just run off, leaving her family and five-year-old son. No. All the indications were that Jessa loved her little boy and had just gotten mixed up with the wrong man—Randall.

He felt Olivia brush her hand over his shoulder, but it took him a moment to realize she'd done that as a gesture of comfort. Apparently, she'd picked up on the vibes he was giving off. Regret over not being able to bring Randall to justice.

"Randall killed Jessa," Leo stated. "There's plenty of circumstantial evidence, but I wasn't able to do what I needed to do to find something more concrete." Maybe Rena could provide that missing piece.

He glanced over to where Olivia still had her hand on his shoulder. But it was bad timing on his part. Because he did that at the exact moment she looked down. His mouth grazed her cheek. And he felt that slight touch in every inch of his body.

Every inch.

Hell. He still wanted her. Bad.

She didn't pull away from him. Instead, Olivia

shifted her gaze so they were staring directly into each other's eyes. Leo could have sworn that the temperature in the room heated up a full twenty degrees, and he fought not to latch onto her and kiss her. It was a battle that he thought he was winning.

When Olivia kissed him.

She made a small sound, a mix of surprise and pleasure. Not good. Because that pleasure kicked his need for her into overdrive. Now, he did latch onto her, turning in the chair so that he could take her mouth the way he wanted. He made the kiss long and deep, more than enough to qualify as foreplay. Foreplay that shouldn't be happening. No way should he be muddying the waters like this with her.

Olivia seemed to agree with him on that last part because she pulled away. Her breathing was way too heavy. Her face flushed. She took several steps back to put some distance between them.

"We should be talking about Randall," Olivia muttered, still fighting to level her breathing. "And about Milton. We shouldn't be kissing."

Leo couldn't argue with any of that. Of course, at the moment, he couldn't speak to argue about anything. It took him several moments to shake off the heat and gather some common sense. The investigation. That should be their focus because the only way to stop the danger was to find the person responsible.

Olivia cleared her throat and sat back down. "Did Randall's alibi check out for the attack?" she asked.

Since she'd managed to get past the kiss, Leo made sure he did, as well. "On the surface." He'd gone through Barrett's report first thing this morning. "His current girlfriend said he was with her, but that doesn't mean he's innocent."

It also didn't mean the girlfriend was telling the truth. Lovers lied for each other all the time. Heck, Olivia had lied to him when she'd ended their relationship. Lied because she hadn't wanted him to incur her father's wrath. Later, it was a discussion that Olivia and he needed to have, but for now he went back to the PI's report on Rena. He'd barely finished the next page before the landline phone rang on Barrett's desk.

"Deputy Logan," Leo answered.

"Deputy Logan," the caller repeated. "Good. I would have called you next. I'm Deputy Chief Trey Mercer from the Culver Crossing Fire Department. I'm trying to reach Olivia Nash."

Leo immediately felt the punch of dread. "She's here. What's wrong?" he demanded, and he put the call on speaker.

"I've got a crew on the way out to her place now," Trey said. "A call came in from an anonymous source about twenty minutes ago, and the person said he'd set fire to her house."

Olivia practically leaped to her feet. "You've verified there really is a fire?" she asked. And Leo knew what she was thinking—that it could be a lure to draw them out.

"Not yet. But the caller said there was a second fire. This one is out of my jurisdiction, though. He claims it's in Mercy Ridge, so I've alerted the fire chief there."

Leo got to his feet, too, just as his own phone rang. "Where in Mercy Ridge?" he snapped.

"According to the call," the deputy chief answered, "there's an incendiary device on a timer, and it's set to go off at your house in ten minutes."

## Chapter Eight

The fear cut through Olivia like a switchblade and, for a second, the air vanished from her lungs. She couldn't catch her breath, but she turned and started out of the office. Leo, right behind her, took hold of her arm before she could bolt out the front door.

"Wait," Leo insisted over the sound of his still ringing phone. "This could be a trap."

Olivia hadn't even thought of that and didn't want to think of it now. She only wanted to get to Cameron and to make sure he was okay.

"What's wrong?" Bernice asked. "Is there trouble?"

Leo didn't respond to the woman, but he did answer his phone. Olivia saw Mercy Ridge Fire Department on his screen. "Are you on your way out to my place?" Leo demanded the moment he had someone on the line.

"Yes," the caller assured him. "Our ETA is about ten minutes."

That felt like an eternity. Way too long to make sure Cameron was safe.

"Get there as fast as you can," Leo insisted.

He ended the call and immediately made another one. This time to Daniel. And he did all that while hanging on to Olivia's hand, probably to ensure that she didn't run outside.

"Daniel," he said when his brother answered. "Culver Crossing PD got an anonymous tip that there could be a device rigged to set a fire at my house. Any signs of trouble?"

"None," Daniel said without hesitation. "We've all been keeping watch, and no one has gotten near the house."

That didn't cause Olivia to breathe any easier because, if there truly was a device, it might not have gone off yet.

"Go get Barrett," Leo told Olivia.

She wanted to leave, to get into the cruiser and head straight to Leo's, but she did as Leo asked and hurried to the hall where there were two interview rooms. Deputy Cassidy was standing guard outside one of them, no doubt where Milton was having his eval with the psychiatrist.

"What's wrong?" the deputy asked.

"There's a problem!" Olivia exclaimed as she threw open the second door where Barrett was questioning Rena.

Barrett clearly saw the alarm on Olivia's face because he was already on his feet. "Wait here," he told Rena before rushing out into the hall with Olivia. "Keep an eye on both Milton and Miss Oldham," he directed the deputy.

Olivia didn't waste any time running back toward Leo. He was still on the phone, but he tossed Barrett a set of keys that he took from the dispatcher's desk. "Let's go," Leo demanded. "I'll fill you in on the way."

Barrett didn't question his brother. He snatched the keys out of the air, and the three of them raced to the cruiser that was still parked directly in front of the station. As they'd done on the drive to the sheriff's office, Leo and she jumped in the back, but this time it was Barrett who got in behind the wheel.

Olivia's pulse was thick and throbbing, making it hard for her to hear, but she caught bits and pieces of the instructions that Leo rattled off to Daniel. *Truck. Car seat. Road.*

"Someone might have put a firebomb at Leo's house," she explained to Barrett when his eyes met hers in the rearview mirror.

That was all the info Barrett needed to hit the siren and the accelerator. They sped away from the sheriff's office. Judging from the way Barrett started firing glances all around them, he must have thought this could be some kind of ruse, as well. If so, it had worked because it'd gotten her and Leo out of the building and on the road where they'd be easier targets.

"Daniel and the hands haven't seen anything

suspicious," Leo relayed to them the moment he'd finished his call. "But we're taking precautions anyway since it's possible that someone planted a device days or even weeks ago before we were on watch."

Oh mercy. She hadn't even considered that, but Olivia certainly considered it now. "Cameron," was all she managed to say.

"He'll be fine," Leo quickly told her, but she saw that the assurance didn't make it to his eyes. He was just as terrified for their baby as she was. "Daniel's moving my truck into the garage, and Izzie will get Cameron into his car seat before they drive out. They won't go far, just about twenty yards from the house, and the hands will guard the truck to make sure no one tries to sneak up on them."

Those were good security measures, and it would prevent Cameron from being in the house in case it did catch fire. But Olivia wasn't sure those measures would be enough.

"Someone could fire shots into the truck," she reminded him.

"No. Because no one will get close enough to do that. The hands are armed with rifles, and they're all good shots. No one will get in position to try to hurt Cameron."

Olivia wanted to latch onto that. Wanted it to be the gospel truth. But there were thick trees along Leo's property line, and a sniper could climb one of those and start firing. Of course, if that happened,

Daniel would almost certainly protect Cameron with his life, but it might not be enough.

*It might not be enough.*

She had to choke back the sob that tried to make its way out of her throat, and she forced herself to keep it together. If she gave in to the fear and panic now, it wouldn't help and in fact could hurt. After all, they needed to be focused on any possible threats waiting for them between here and Leo's place.

Leo's phone rang again, the sound shooting through the cruiser. Shooting through her, as well. Olivia's gaze automatically flew to the cell's screen where she expected to see Daniel's name. But it wasn't. It was the Culver Crossing Fire Department again. Leo answered the call right away and put it on speaker.

"It's Deputy Chief Trey Mercer," the caller said. "I've got some bad news."

Olivia could have sworn her heart stopped. Just stopped. A thousand thoughts went through her head, none good.

"We're out at Olivia Nash's place," the fireman continued, "and we're not going to be able to save it. The roof's already collapsed, and the fire's spread into the yard. My men are working to contain it now."

Under most circumstances, Olivia would have found that new devasting, but it was a relief because the *bad news* didn't involve Cameron. She was finally able to release the breath that was now burning in her chest.

"Are you on your way out here?" the fireman asked.

It was Leo who answered. "No. I'm not sure when Olivia will be able to get there. Days, maybe. She's in protective custody."

"Oh." Judging from his surprised tone, the deputy chief hadn't expected that. "All right, then. I'll send you my preliminary report when I can get it done. It'll take a while, though, because this is definitely an arson investigation. There's a strong smell of accelerant."

She hadn't doubted that the fire had been intentionally set. But why? Was it just another distraction, or had their attackers thought she was there? Obviously, someone had wanted to set her up to take the blame for Leo's murder, but maybe she was now the primary target. Or else someone wanted them to believe that.

Leo's phone dinged again with a text message. "It's from Daniel," he said to Barrett and her. "The fire department is at the house, and there are still no signs of a device. The bomb squad's on the way."

Olivia grasped the part about there being *no signs of a device*. The seconds ticked by slowly, and she moved to the edge of her seat as Barrett took the turn to Leo's ranch. It wouldn't be long now before she could see Cameron and, better yet, get him in the cruiser so he'd be better protected. However, the house was still out of view when Barrett slammed on his brakes, sending the tires screeching on the asphalt.

Olivia immediately saw why Barrett had done that. There was a man in the middle of the road, and he was waving his hands around as if trying to flag them down. There was a truck behind him, from which he'd likely made a quick exit because the driver's door was still open.

"Randall," Leo snarled. "What the hell does he want?"

That revved her heartbeat up again. Olivia hadn't recognized the man, though she'd seen his photo in the news during the investigation of his missing girlfriend. Unlike the picture that'd been taken at a party where he'd been dressed in a suit, today he was in jeans and had an unbuttoned denim shirt over a white tee.

Randall was also armed with a rifle.

Barrett didn't lower the window but instead spoke to Randall through the microphone that he unclipped from the siren. "Stop where you are and put down your weapon," he ordered when Randall came closer.

Randall didn't stop. Just the opposite. With both hands gripped on the rifle, he began to run toward the cruiser.

"Get down," Leo told her. He drew his gun. Barrett did the same.

Olivia didn't want to get down. She wanted to

hurry to the ranch to check on Cameron, especially since Randall could be there to set off the timer on any firebomb he might have planted. But there was no way they could ignore this threat that was coming right at them.

Barrett got out and, using the cruiser door for cover, took aim. Leo did the same on the other side of the vehicle.

"Stop," Barrett shouted out again.

However, the moment Barrett gave that command, the blast tore through the air. Not a gunshot. No. This was an explosion, and Randall's truck became a fireball.

THE BLAST CAUSED the cruiser doors to slam into Leo and Barrett. Leo cursed and nearly dropped from the pain when the door caught his injured arm. But he forced himself to stay on his feet. to focus. And to assess what the hell was going on.

Barrett was cursing in pain, too, because his door had rammed into his shoulder. Randall was on the ground where he'd landed face-first. His rifle was no longer in his hands, probably because it'd been thrown clear from him in the fall. That was the good news, that Randall was no longer armed. Good, too, that Olivia wasn't hurt—Leo glanced at her to see that she was shaken up, but she hadn't been injured.

The bad news was that pieces of Randall's truck were raining down around them. Fiery bits of metal and rubber that could be just as deadly as bullets.

"Get back in the cruiser," Leo told his brother, and he did the same. He got another jolt of pain from his arm when he had to use his hand to slam the door shut.

In the front, Barrett did the same, and he grabbed the microphone again. "Randall, if you can move, take cover under the cruiser. There could be a secondary explosion from the gas tank."

Randall lifted his head, shook it as if to clear it and, with plenty of effort, got to a crouching position. He was bleeding. Leo couldn't tell how badly he was hurt because the black smoke billowing off what was left of his truck immediately engulfed him.

"You tried to kill me!" Randall shouted. "So help you, you Logans will pay for this."

Obviously, Randall thought they were responsible for whatever had caused his truck to explode. It was possible, though, that this was some kind of sick plan to make himself look innocent. If so, the ploy had clearly gotten out of hand. He could have been killed.

Randall came out of the smoke, walking now. Or rather, stumbling and limping. But he didn't move toward the cruiser. Instead, he made his way to the side of the road, dropped down into the ditch and headed for a cluster of trees. What he hadn't done was pick up his rifle. It was still on the ground.

"I'll call for assistance," Barrett said, using the phone on the dash as he put the cruiser in Reverse.

"I can't get past the fire, so I'll have to use the ranch trail."

The trail would indeed get them to the house, but it would take longer than the road. Plus, there was the huge concern that someone might be lying in wait along the route since his ranch hands weren't patrolling that particular area of his property.

Leo took out his phone to call Daniel, but it rang in his hand and he saw his brother's name on the screen.

"We heard a blast," Daniel said the moment Leo answered. "Are you all okay?"

"Yeah. What about Cameron, Izzie and you?" Leo countered.

"Fine. What blew up?"

"Randall's truck. He wasn't in it at the time, so he's still alive," Leo added, and he glanced in the direction where he'd last seen the man. He was no longer in sight. "The road isn't passable right now, so we'll use the west trail. Our ETA is about ten minutes. Eight," he amended when Barrett hit the accelerator and got them speeding out of there.

"Any idea who blew up Randall's truck?" Daniel asked.

"Not yet. Maybe Randall himself. Possibly the person who hired Milton. Just keep Cameron safe," Leo stressed.

"Will do. See you in a few."

Leo ended the call and turned to Olivia to do another check on her. She was way paler than usual, but she looked a lot steadier than he'd thought she would be.

"You're hurt," she muttered, reaching for his sleeve that now had some blood on it. The impact of the cruiser door had obviously reopened the wound.

"I'll clean it when I get home," he assured her, hoping there'd be a home for him to go back to.

Until he'd seen Randall's truck get blown to bits, Leo hadn't been sure there truly was a device rigged with an explosive. Obviously, there had been, and now he could only pray there wasn't a second device. Especially one anywhere near Cameron that someone else could set off.

Olivia didn't listen to his comment about taking care of the wound when he got home. She eased up his sleeve and had a look for herself. Leo didn't glance down when she started to dab away the blood. He kept his attention on the turn that Barrett made onto the trail.

Unlike the main road, the west trail was narrow, only wide enough for one vehicle. Along with plenty of potholes in the gravel surface, it was lined on both sides with trees and thick underbrush. Plenty of places for someone to hide, though Leo didn't think they had to worry about Randall. Even if the man had managed to run at full speed, he wouldn't have been able to get here and set up position for an attack.

Going as fast as he safely could, Barrett sped down the trail, hitting his breaks to take a deep curve. The moment he did, Leo heard a sound he definitely didn't want to hear.

A gunshot.

Hell. This was exactly what Leo had feared would happen. And what he'd hoped they could avoid.

The first bullet didn't hit the cruiser, but the second one did. It slammed into the front of the vehicle, and Leo immediately pushed Olivia down onto the seat. He also glanced around, looking for the shooter.

And he soon found him.

There was a man just ahead, leaning out from a spindly tree. He wasn't wearing a mask, so Leo saw his face but didn't recognize him. A stranger. That meant this was likely a hired gun.

"Hold on," Barrett warned a split second before he aimed the cruiser in the direction of the shooter.

Obviously, the guy hadn't been expecting that because he scrambled out of the way before he could get off another shot. Barrett slammed on his brakes, the side of the cruiser scraping against the tree.

Leo already had his weapon ready. So did Barrett. They fired glances around, looking to see if this idiot was alone or if he'd brought backup. Leo didn't see anyone else.

The moment the cruiser stopped, Leo and Barrett threw open their doors, both taking aim at the gunman who was still trying to get his balance.

"I'm Sheriff Logan," Barrett called out. "Drop your weapon and put up your hands or I'll shoot."

The man whirled around and in the same motion, brought up his gun. Definitely not a move to drop the weapon as Barrett had ordered. And Leo got confirmation of that when the man fired a shot at them. Leo had no doubts that this idiot would kill all of them if he got the chance. And that's why Leo pulled the trigger. He aimed for the guy's chest and sent two rounds into him.

That stopped him.

The man froze, the look of shock washing over his face. He dropped his gun so he could clasp his hands to his chest. Not that it would do any good. No. Leo could see that the guy was bleeding out fast.

"Call an ambulance," Leo told Olivia, tossing her his phone.

Maybe, just maybe, they could keep this SOB alive so he could tell them what the hell was going on.

## Chapter Nine

Olivia made the call for the EMTs to come to the ranch trail to try to save the man who'd just tried to kill them. Maybe the same man who'd also blown up Randall's truck. If they got lucky, he'd be able to tell them for himself.

"Take the cruiser and get Olivia out of here so you can check on Cameron," Barrett instructed Leo. "I'll wait here until the ambulance arrives."

Leo shook his head and glanced around. "I don't want to leave you alone because this guy could have a partner or two."

Barrett made a sound of agreement. "And if he does, he'll be going after Olivia and you. Take her to your house, and move Cameron and the nanny into the cruiser where they'll be safer. Then, all of you can go back to the sheriff's office until we get the all-clear on your place."

Olivia also had worries about leaving Barrett, but she was desperate to see her son and to make sure he was okay.

"All of you can bunk in the breakroom until we figure out a better place," Barrett added and then motioned for Leo to move. "Go ahead. Get Olivia away from this."

Leo nodded, but there was a lot of hesitancy in his expression. However, he finally got behind the wheel and took off. He also called Daniel and gave him a brief explanation as to what was going on and asked that Daniel come to assist Barrett as soon as Olivia and he were back at the ranch. It wasn't a great plan because any or all of them could be in danger from a sniper, but at the moment he had no great plan other than to make things as safe for Cameron as he could.

Olivia dug her fingers into the seat as Leo maneuvered the cruiser through the snaking trail. She also kept watch, praying that there wasn't a second gunman. Thankfully, she didn't see anyone until they reached the edge of the ranch, and she recognized the man as one of Leo's hands. He gave Leo a nod of greeting and continued to stand guard.

"Don't get out until I'm right next to the truck," Leo told her, figuring that she would indeed scramble to see Cameron.

Olivia obeyed, but she put her hand on the door, ready to open it, and waited for Leo to park side by side with his truck. Daniel must have been ready, too, because Leo and he moved as if they'd rehearsed it. Within seconds, both Izzie and Cameron were in the back seat of the cruiser with Olivia.

She immediately took her son from his seat and into her arms.

Cameron was smiling and babbled some happy sounds, so he obviously wasn't aware of what was going on. Good. She wanted to shelter him as much as she could. For now, Olivia showered him with kisses and lifted him when Leo looked back at the boy. Cameron had a big smile for him, too, and reached out for his dad to take him, but Leo just gave him a kiss and ruffled his hair.

"He needs to go back in his seat," Leo instructed. "I don't want to stay here in case the place explodes."

Izzie didn't gasp, but Olivia saw the nanny's bottom lip trembling. "Daniel told you what's going on?" Olivia asked and got a nod. "We'll be okay," Olivia tried to reassure her.

While Olivia strapped Cameron back in, Daniel hurried over to the truck, no doubt to go to Barrett. Leo also made a call and, within just a couple of minutes, two of his hands drove up in a dark blue truck.

"They'll follow us back to the sheriff's office," Leo advised, driving away the moment she and Izzie had on their seat belts. "We can't go out the main road because of Randall's truck, and we can't use the west trail since Daniel and the ambulance will have that way blocked. We'll have to go through the trail that leads off the back pasture."

Olivia was grateful for the backup and hoped it

would be enough. She didn't want the reassurance she'd just given Izzie to be lip service.

Leo's gaze met hers in the mirror for a split second. Maybe he was trying to dole out some encouragement, too, but Olivia also took it as a signal to keep watch. After all, there could also be another sniper on this trail.

And that caused her to consider something.

Even if the person behind these attacks hadn't actually paid Milton, he or she would have likely had to pay the wounded man on the trail. Perhaps had to pay others, as well. She doubted payments like that would be cheap.

That brought her back to Randall and her father.

They had the kind of money to order a hit and to create this kind of chaos. Rena did not. Olivia didn't know if Bernice did, either, but if money was a factor here, it'd rule out Rena. Then again, money could be borrowed or stolen, and services could be bartered or coerced. In other words, any one of their suspects could have pulled this off.

Olivia pushed all of that aside and continued to keep watch. Every few seconds, she also checked on Cameron. It was still too early for his morning nap, but his eyelids were getting droopy. so it was possible he'd sleep through the rest of this horrible ordeal.

It took nearly twenty minutes for Leo to thread his way through the rough trail and back to the road, and he did so by using his hands-free set on the cruiser to make some calls. One was to the dispatcher to report that Randall had been injured and had run from the scene. He asked that an APB be put out on the man.

When they passed by what was left of Randall's truck, she spotted the fire department and the bomb squad. Good. Once they finished with the burned-out vehicle, then they could check Leo's place.

"Daniel said your house burned," she heard Izzie say. "I'm so sorry."

Olivia wasn't surprised she'd actually forgotten about that. It was a loss, not the house itself, but the things she had in it. Her photos, Cameron's favorite toys, and the cedar chest filled with things that had once belonged to her mother—jewelry, photos and even her journals. She was certain that later she'd feel the sting of losing those things, but it was hard to feel loss when her son's safety was her priority. Thankfully, it was Leo's priority, as well.

"Thank you," Olivia murmured to Izzie just as Leo pulled to a stop in front of the sheriff's office.

Deputy Cassidy was in the doorway, clearly waiting for them, which meant Barrett had likely alerted her. "This way," she said once Olivia had Cameron out of the cruiser. She kept him in his car seat since he was not only sound asleep now but because the seat would also better protect him if someone fired shots at them.

But no shots came.

Olivia said a quick prayer of thanks for that and

was also relieved that neither Rena nor Bernice was in the large front office space. It was empty except for another deputy, a lanky built man, who was now at the dispatch desk.

"Where are Milton, Rena and Bernice?" Leo asked, glancing around but aiming his question at Deputy Cassidy.

"Milton's back in his cell. The psychiatrist finished with him and left about twenty minutes ago. Barrett told Rena and Bernice to leave after the trouble at your place. He said he'd reschedule their interviews."

Olivia wasn't sure when Barrett would find time to squeeze that in since he now had a new facet of the investigation. One that involved a firebomb that'd destroyed Randall's truck. That reminder that her wondering where the man was.

Even though it was maybe too early for the APB to have gone into effect, Olivia turned to the deputy. "Any sign of Randall?"

Deputy Cassidy shook her head. "Nothing yet. And call me Cybil. I've tried to call Randall twice, but it goes straight to voice mail. Could be he's just trying to avoid being brought in for questioning."

True, but the man had been hurt. "I'm guessing you checked the hospital?"

Cybil nodded. "The one here and the one in Culver Crossing. He hasn't gone to either." She led them through the hall and toward the back of the building. "Barrett asked me to fix up the breakroom as best I could."

Even though she'd visited Leo several times at work when they'd still been together, Olivia had never been to this part of the sheriff's office, and it wasn't as bad as she'd expected. It was actually two spacious rooms, one with bunkbeds, probably for anyone who got stuck pulling long shifts. The main room had a well-worn brown-leather sofa, a TV, some lockers and even a small kitchenette. It smelled like coffee and the cinnamon bagels that were in a plastic bag on the counter.

The place looked safe enough what with the wired-glass window, but it gave Olivia an uneasy feeling to know that they were now under the same roof as Milton.

"I changed the sheets on the beds," the deputy told Leo, and he muttered a thanks. "Wasn't sure how long you'd have to be here, but I thought you'd need a place to sleep," she added, shifting her attention to Olivia. "The sheriff said you might need someone to get baby supplies."

Olivia had no idea and had to look at Izzie for the answer. The nanny had brought the diaper bag, but Olivia didn't know what she'd managed to stuff in there before they'd had to evacuate the house.

"We're okay for now," Izzie replied. "But if we're still here tomorrow, we'll need extra diapers, wipes and some baby food."

"Just give me a list and I'll get whatever you

need," the deputy assured her. She pointed to the door on the left side of the sofa. "That's a small bathroom with a shower. Maybe you'll want to get that blood off you. You, too," she added to Leo.

Olivia glanced down at her top and saw there was indeed blood. She'd probably gotten it when she'd examined the wound on Leo's arm. There was blood on his shirt, as well.

"You need an EMT to take a look at that?" Cybil asked him.

"No." He answered fast while taking the infant seat with Cameron from Olivia. "I've got a first-aid kit and a change of clothes in my locker. There's also an extra shirt in there for Olivia."

Olivia nearly asked if someone could go by her place to pick up some of her own clothes, but then she remembered that the only clothing she owned was what she was wearing.

"Why don't I take Cameron into the bunkroom so he can finish his nap?" Izzie suggested when Cybil left. "That'll give you two a chance to change and redress that wound."

Neither Leo nor Olivia objected. If Cameron woke up, she didn't want him to see the bloody clothes. Plus, Olivia needed some time to steady herself. She wasn't sure that was actually possible, not with the adrenaline still pumping through her, but she had to try.

Once Izzie and Cameron were in the bunkroom, the nanny eased the door shut. Leo must have taken that as his cue to get started with their "chores" because he went to his locker and took out a small first-aid kit along with two shirts, one a black tee and the other a pale blue button-up. He tossed the blue one to her and shucked off his bloody shirt.

He also winced.

Leo had probably hoped to cover that up, but Olivia saw it, all right. On a heavy sigh, she went to him. "Let me clean that wound before you put on the T-shirt."

That would make it easier to deal with the gash, but of course, it also meant she'd have her hands on a bare-chested Leo. Considering their earlier kiss and the steamy attraction that was always there between them, that probably wasn't a bright idea, but his injury needed some tending.

"I need to text Barrett first to make sure he's okay," Leo muttered.

She waited for him to do that, waited some more for a response from Barrett, who confirmed all was well and that the signs were that the gunman had been working alone. Barrett added that he'd call as soon as he had more info.

With that weight off Leo's mind, Olivia had him sit on the sofa as she looked through the kit to find some fresh bandages, antiseptic cream and gauze pads. She wet a couple of the pads in the sink in the bathroom so she could wash away some of the blood. The wound had, indeed, reopened, and it was red. It had to be hurting him.

"You really should see an EMT again," she said, frowning when she saw him grimace in pain.

"It'll be fine. It's not that deep of a cut."

It really wasn't, and it would almost certainly heal on its own if he kept it clean and didn't flex the muscles beneath it. She could make sure the first happened but not the second. If they came under attack again, she knew that Leo would definitely do some *flexing* to protect Cameron and her.

She sank next to him on the sofa to apply the fresh bandage and felt him shudder when the back of her hand brushed against his chest. Olivia lifted her gaze to apologize for hurting him, but then she realized Leo's wince wasn't from pain.

No.

There was some heat in his eyes. Heat spurred by her touch. Maybe other things were playing into this, too. After all, they'd just survived nearly being killed, which had almost certainly left them as raw as the cut on his arm.

"You keep saving me," she said, her voice thick.

She hadn't intended for it to sound like a whispery come-on, but it did. No doubt because she had been affected by that touch, as well. And just by being this close to Leo. His scent was like foreplay to her. Ditto for his incredible face. It didn't help when the corner of his equally incredible mouth lifted into a near smile.

"At least this gets your mind off the fire and the

attack," he drawled. That voice was like foreplay, as well.

"It gets your mind off things, too," she countered, figuring that would jar him back into remembering that the last thing they should be doing was looking at each other like this.

Olivia had no trouble remembering that. Still, she stayed put and didn't take her eyes off him. She didn't move, either, when he leaned in and brushed his mouth over hers. It seemed to be some kind of test to see how she'd react. Or maybe how *he* would react. Apparently, not good, because he squeezed his eyes shut a moment and ground out some profanity.

That's why she was shocked when his mouth came back to hers.

This time, it wasn't just a touch. It was a scalding kiss that sent a wave of fiery need straight to the center of her body. That was the problem with kissing a former lover, one she was still seriously attracted to—the heat instantly skyrocketed and made her want to do a whole lot more than just kiss him.

Leo accommodated her on the *more*. He hooked his uninjured arm around her and pulled her to him. Olivia landed against his bare chest. That definitely didn't help cool things down any.

Her pulse kicked up a notch, and she couldn't stop herself from sliding deeper into the kiss. Or stop herself from touching him. She slid her hands around his back and gave herself the thrill of feeling all those taut, toned muscles respond to her touch. Then again, Leo had always responded to her.

And was responding now.

The sound he made was one of pure need. An ache so strong that it seemed to come off him in thick, hot waves and wash over her. She fought to get closer to him, adjusting her position so that her breasts moved over his chest. Another thrill. More fuel for this blistering heat that'd make her crazy if it didn't stop.

Leo must have remembered where they were and that anyone could come walking in at any second because he broke the kiss. He didn't move back, though. He sat there, his breath gusting, his forehead pressed against hers.

The air was so still, it felt as if everything was on hold, waiting. Olivia was certainly waiting for his reaction, to see if he would be disgusted with himself. However, it wasn't disgust on his face when he finally pulled back and locked eyes with her. The heat and need were still there, still eating away at him as it did her.

"Well, at least you have a foolproof way of making me forget about the fires and danger for a couple of seconds," she murmured.

He smiled. And, mercy, it was good to see it. It'd been so long since she'd seen Leo happy. Even though she doubted he was actually happy right now. He'd just grabbed on to something to anchor himself and create a distraction. She understood that because the kiss had shaken her to the core.

"When I kiss you like that," he said, his voice husky, "I have a hard time remembering that we're not together. And an equally hard time remembering why we broke up."

She had the same problem. But she didn't get a chance to tell him that because his phone rang and she saw Barrett's name on the screen. That got Leo moving away from her. He hit the button to put the call on speaker and set down his phone long enough to slip on the black T-shirt.

"Everything okay there?" Barrett asked.

"Yeah," Leo answered and then quickly followed with a question of his own. "Did they find a fire-bomb at my house?"

"No. Not yet anyway. That's the good news. The bad news is that the shooter died before the EMTs arrived. He never regained consciousness, so I couldn't question him. His wallet was in his pocket, though, so I got his driver's license. His name was Lowell Jensen."

Leo's forehead bunched. "That sounds familiar."

It rang a bell for Olivia, too, but it took her a moment to figure out where she'd heard it. Or rather, had seen it. "I'm pretty sure a Lowell Jansen was in the PI report that Bernice gave us. Lowell was one of Rena's ex-lovers and he has—*had*—" she amended, "a police record."

"That report is in your office," Leo interjected. "I'll go get it."

"That can wait a couple of minutes. What I'll need you to do is arrange to have Rena brought back in. I'd let her go when all hell broke loose out at your place, but I want to ask her about this."

"I'll also look for any money trail," Leo noted. "But if he's her ex, then maybe she didn't pay him with money. It could be she used sex, or maybe he was just doing a favor for her."

The anger rolled over Olivia again and she hoped that this time when they questioned Rena, the woman broke down and confessed. If she were guilty, that was. Since someone had used her own phone to set her up, Olivia knew that things weren't often as they seemed on the surface.

"There's more," Barrett went on. "We found Lowell's Jeep just off the trail, and there were some things in it that might have been taken from Olivia's house. It was a bag with her mother's journals."

Olivia drew in a sharp breath. "Yes, they were at my house." But she had to mentally shake her head. "Why'd he take those?"

"I was hoping you'd have the answer to that. And, no, I'm not accusing you of anything," Barrett quickly added. "I just wondered if you had any ideas as to why someone would want to steal them and only them. There was nothing else of yours in the Jeep."

Olivia forced away the fog from the spent adrenaline and the kiss, and tried to make sense of it. She couldn't. "The journals, all thirteen of them, were right next to some of my mother's jewelry. Some of the pieces were worth a lot of money and looked it, too. By that I mean anyone who saw them would know they were valuable."

Barrett didn't ask her why such pieces weren't in a safe or a safe-deposit box, and Olivia was thankful for it. She didn't want to explain that she'd needed to keep close what few things she had of her mother's. It was a way of remembering her and not just the car wreck that'd claimed her life. However, there was something about the journals she thought he should know.

"I made digital copies of the journals," she told him. "Just in case something happened and they were damaged or destroyed. I knew that wouldn't be the same thing as having the originals in her own handwriting, but it was a way to preserve her memories."

Especially since those journals were something Simone had devoted plenty of time to keeping up. Her mother hadn't written in them daily, not even weekly, but there were at least a couple of entries every month.

"Any chance there's something in the journals that could connect to what's going on now with the attacks?" Barrett prompted.

She opened her mouth to say an automatic no but then rethought that. "I don't think so. I mean…

I've read every entry multiple times." Some, like the ones her mother had written days following Olivia's birth, she'd read hundreds of times. "They have great sentimental value to me, of course, but my mother didn't say anything in them that would hint of a crime or such."

At least, she didn't think Simone had, but once she got her hands on them again, Olivia wouldn't mind taking another look. It'd been years since she'd actually looked through any of the entries.

"All right," Barrett said a moment later. "I'll have to take the journals into custody as evidence for a while, but I'll see that you get them back."

She muttered a heartfelt thanks just as an incoming call flashed on Leo's screen. It was from her father.

Olivia could see the hesitation pass through Leo's eyes. He was likely considering if he should just let the call go to voice mail. However, he must have decided against that.

"Samuel's calling," Leo explained to his brother. "Let me see what he wants and I'll get back to you."

Leo switched over to her father, but he took a deep breath before he said anything. "I'm busy," Leo snapped. "Make it quick."

"Where are Cameron and Olivia?" Samuel fired back.

"They're safe," Leo assured him while also dodging the question. "And if that's why you called, this conversation is over—"

"It's not the only reason I called." Her father was talking quickly, his words running together, probably because he thought Leo might just hang up on him. "I'm at Olivia's house now, and it's been burned to the ground. I heard the firemen talking, and they said it was arson. What they wouldn't tell me was if Olivia and Cameron were inside when the place caught fire."

Leo sighed. "They weren't in the house. They're okay."

"I need to see them," he insisted. "I need to see you."

"Me?" Leo snarled. "Why?"

"I take it you haven't gotten a call about it yet?"

Her father's question had Leo glancing at her to see if she knew what he was talking about. She didn't.

"Explain that," Leo ordered. "And just know, if this is some kind of scheme so you can try to see Olivia and Cameron, then I'll arrest you for impeding an investigation."

"It's not a scheme," her father insisted. He muttered a curse. "Someone just called me from an unknown number. I didn't recognize the voice, but the person said I was to go to Olivia's house and look for…something."

"Something?" Leo questioned.

"A body," Samuel said after a long pause. "The caller said that someone had been murdered."

## Chapter Ten

"A body," Olivia murmured.

Even though her voice was barely audible, Leo could hear the fresh worry. And the fear.

Hell. Would this never end?

Leo was about to tell Samuel—and maybe reassure Olivia in the process—that the anonymous call to report a murder could be bogus. A foolish prank by someone who'd heard the news reports of the attack and just wanted to stir up trouble. But his phone dinged with another incoming call and his gut tightened when he saw the name on the screen.

Sheriff Jace Castillo.

Without saying anything else to Samuel, Jace hung up on him and switched over to Jace. He also slid his arm around Olivia. Coming on the heels of that kiss, touching her probably wasn't a good thing, but he hated the look this had put back in her eyes. She was having too much dumped on her too fast, and he didn't want her caving into the fear.

"Let me guess," Leo greeted when Jace was on

the line. "You got a report about a body being out at Olivia's?"

"I did," Jace verified. "I'm on my way there now. Do you have ESP or did you get a call, too?"

"Not me, but Samuel did. Any chance the caller told you specifically where to look for this body?" Leo prompted.

"No. I guess he or she didn't want to make it too easy for me. And I didn't have any luck tracing the call, either. The person was using a burner cell."

That didn't surprise Leo. But the first part of what Jace had said did catch his attention. *"He or she?"*

Jace made a sound of agreement. "The caller's voice was muffled. Not like through a scrambler. It was much more low-tech than that. Probably a cloth or hand held over the mouthpiece."

"Samuel didn't say anything about that, but if he's still at Olivia's place when you get there, you'll want to ask him about it."

"Oh, believe me, I will. If I miss him, I'll bring him in for questioning. And won't that be fun?" Jace added in a grumble.

Leo nearly smiled. Nearly. Jace and he didn't have much in common, but apparently they both had an extreme dislike for Olivia's father.

There was a sound from the bunkroom—one that Leo quickly recognized. Cameron was fussing about something. Olivia untangled herself from his arms and hurried in that direction. Leo looked in, as well, but Cameron was just having a finicky spell after waking from his short nap.

"Any chance this caller mentioned to Samuel the identity of this DB I'm supposed to be looking for?" Jace asked.

"He didn't say, but it could be someone connected to the arsonist." Since Leo didn't want Cameron to hear any part of this, he stepped back into the breakroom. "Or maybe he was the arsonist." This could all be tied together with the other attacks. "You've heard about the dead gunman near my place?"

"I did," Jace confirmed. "Also heard that someone rigged it so that your house would go up in flames, too."

"Nothing so far," Leo assured him, and hoped it stayed that way. Not just because the ranch was his and Cameron's home but also because it'd been in his family for several generations. Still, the house was something he could rebuild if it came down to it. The important thing was to keep Cameron safe.

And Olivia.

Somehow, she had become as important as Cameron in that "keep safe" equation. It was because of the kisses and the damn heat that just wouldn't go away. But it was more than that, too. It wasn't just his body that was revving up for her again. No. The rest of him had gotten in on it, as well, and he knew without a doubt that he was falling hard for her again.

That meant Olivia would have a second chance to crush his heart.

It was really bad timing for that thought to pop into his head, so he forced it aside. Not just for the moment, either, but he told his body to knock it off, to stop thinking about anything but the investigation that would hopefully lead to them all being safe. Because right now, the danger wasn't just limited to Olivia, Cameron and him. Anyone caught in the crosshairs of these attacks could be hurt or worse.

"I'll let you know if I find anything at Olivia's," he heard Jace say, and that helped snap Leo the rest of the way back.

Leo thanked him, ended the call and just stared at his phone for several more seconds. His "knock it off" lecture to himself had apparently paid up because he started mentally ticking off things he should be doing. And none of those things involved kissing Olivia or thinking about kissing her.

"Are you okay?" Olivia asked, touching his arm to get his attention. He'd been so lost in thought that he hadn't heard her come back into the room.

Leo nodded and put his phone away. "How's Cameron?"

"Cranky. Izzie's taking out the toys from the diaper bag. That should distract him."

Maybe, but Leo couldn't imagine there were a lot of things for the boy to play with in that bag. If he couldn't take Cameron home to his place soon, then he'd need to have some brought here.

"I'm going to Barrett's office to get the envelope Bernice gave us, a laptop and any other files that I think will help me start sorting out some details of this case," Leo explained, tipping his head to the table where many of the deputies often ate lunch. "I can work there."

She glanced in at Cameron, who was indeed occupied, for the moment anyway, with a book. "I'll go with you and help you bring back the stuff." She relayed that to Izzie and followed Leo down the hall to Barrett's office.

Cybil was back at the dispatch desk, and she looked up when they came in. "Everything okay?" It was obvious she was on full alert because she shifted as if she might have to spring to action.

Leo shook his head. "Just need some things." He went into the office, handed the envelope and some other files to Olivia, and grabbed two laptops. One he took from Barrett's desk and the other from his own. "You can read through some reports," he said to Olivia. "It wouldn't hurt to have a fresh eye on them. Plus, there'll be reports coming in from Culver Crossing."

Reports on the fire that had destroyed her house. Maybe even one on the "body" that Jace was looking for. She welcomed the task because it would make her feel as if she were actually doing something to help. However, they hadn't even started back to the breakroom when the front door opened and Barrett walked in.

The brothers' gazes met and held for a few seconds, and she thought that maybe they were assessing to make sure each was okay. Barrett frowned when he saw the fresh bandage on Leo's arm.

"Olivia couldn't talk you into having an EMT check that out?" Barrett asked.

"No," she answered on a sigh just as Leo said, "It's fine."

Leo tipped his head to the evidence bags in Barrett's hand. "Is that what you got from the dead gunman?"

Barrett nodded, but he sighed, too, probably because he knew that Leo had just shut him down on the possibility of getting medical treatment. "I have his phone. A burner," Barrett added, "so I don't expect we'll get much." He shifted to show the other bag, a much larger one with a form attached to it. Since it was clear plastic, Olivia could see what was inside.

Her mother's journals.

No mistaking those distinct Tiffany-blue covers or the size. Not large notebook journals but rather more the dimensions of slim diaries. Each of the thirteen had only fifty pages, and her mother had filled those pages front and back.

She automatically moved to take them but then remembered they were now evidence. Evidence that might somehow help them unravel this case.

Well, it would if they got lucky and figured out why a now-dead arsonist/would-be killer would have taken them in the first place. Olivia was giving that more thought when she saw someone approaching the sheriff's office. And she groaned.

"My dad's here," she warned Leo and Barrett. Obviously, he'd driven straight over from her place after he'd called Leo.

Both Leo and Barrett adjusted their positions, stepping so that they were like a shield in front of her. Leo took it one step further. He put the laptops on the nearest desk to free up his hands. One of those hands he slid over the weapon in his holster.

Olivia wanted to think that wasn't necessary, that her father wouldn't harm her, but with the memories of the latest attack still right at the front of her mind, she didn't have a lot of trust for him right now.

"I figured you'd be here," Samuel said and, as usual, he threw a glare at Leo. One at Barrett, too.

Maybe Leo was also feeling distrustful of her father because he slipped his free arm around her, easing her behind him. It wasn't a gesture that her father missed. She hadn't thought it possible for him to narrow his eyes even more, but that did it.

"Olivia, please tell me you're not thinking about getting back together with him," her father snarled, adding some extra venom when he said the word *him*.

She thought of the kisses. The heat. The intimacy that was now between them because they were working to solve this case and to keep Cameron safe.

But it was more than just the investigation.

Her feelings for Leo were as strong as ever, and she wasn't sure there was a reason to continue putting up barriers to keep them apart. Her father had created those barriers by threatening to ruin Leo, and maybe he would follow through with those threats. Or perhaps he'd try to do worse if he was the one behind the attacks. But she still couldn't see that as a reason to shut Leo out. It was past time that she dealt with her father head-on.

"It's none of your business whether I'm with Leo or not," she said. Olivia made sure it sounded like the warning it was. "In fact, nothing I do is any concern of yours."

He flinched, as if she'd actually slapped him. Her father stayed quiet a moment, but she could see the anger simmering. Anger that he might have intended to aim at Leo. However, his attention landed on Barrett. Specifically, on the large evidence bag that Barrett was still holding. He flinched again, but this seemed different than his reaction to what she'd said.

"Those are your mother's diaries," Samuel murmured, glancing at her before turning back to Barrett. "What are you doing with those?" he demanded.

"They're potential evidence," Barrett said. His voice was calm, but after one glance, Olivia could see that he was studying her father. Leo was, too. "The man who tried to kill Olivia, Leo and me apparently stole them from Olivia's house. Would you happen to know anything about that?"

Her father's shoulders went back, and it seemed to her that he changed his mind as to what he'd been about to say. "You kept them?" he demanded from her.

Of all the questions she'd thought he might ask, that wasn't one of them. She nodded. "After she died, I went into her office and got them. She used to let me read some of the entries she'd made when she was pregnant with me, so I knew where she kept them."

They'd been in a small wooden storage box on her bookshelf. It had looked like part of the rest of the decor in her office except this particular box had a false bottom. Her mom had called it her private place to keep her secrets. Others had known about the journals, of course, since they'd seen her mom writing in them from time to time. Obviously, her father had known for him to have instantly recognized them.

"Why would someone steal them?" Samuel asked, and his confusion seemed genuine.

*Seemed.*

"You shouldn't have kept them," he continued without waiting for an answer. "All they can do is stir up old, bad memories."

Well, that seemed to be what they were doing

for him. And that brought Olivia right back to the doubts and suspicions she'd been having about him.

"Did you drug my mother the night of her car accident?" Olivia came out and asked. "Are you the reason she's dead?"

Clearly, she'd shocked Barrett because he glanced at her and then, obviously wanting to hear the answer, turned his cop's stare on Samuel. But her father was well beyond being stunned. His jaw went slack, and she didn't think it was her imagination that he lost some color. Or stopped breathing. Her breath had even seemed to have stalled in her chest.

"You think I killed Simone?" he finally managed to say. There was no anger in his voice. Hurt maybe. But oh, the anger came. Olivia saw it flare in his eyes. "You think I risked your life by drugging her?"

"I don't believe you thought I'd be in the car," she countered and then repeated a variation of her question. "Did you drug Mom because you wanted to get her out of your life?"

The anger in his eyes went up a huge notch. "No," he answered despite his jaw being set as hard as stone. "I've never killed anyone, and I never gave your mother any drugs."

"Her tox screen proved she had drugs in her blood," Leo quickly pointed out.

Samuel shifted that stony look to Leo. "Well, she didn't get them from me. Is this some kind of witch hunt?" Samuel volleyed glances at all of them before he settled on staring at her.

Leo shook his head. "No. We're just after the truth, and that's the reason I'm planning to ask the Texas Rangers to reopen the investigation into Simone's death. Who knows—maybe there's something in those journals that'll help them find out what really happened that night."

The anger was a raging storm inside her father now, practically coming off him in thick, hot waves. This was a man who could kill, she realized. This was a man who could have drugged his wife and gotten away with murder.

"If there's anything in Simone's journals that points to me, then she had it wrong," Samuel decreed.

"She wanted a divorce," Olivia said. She'd heard enough of their argument that night to know that.

Her father certainly didn't jump to deny it. In fact, he lifted his shoulder in what he probably thought was a casual dismissal, but his muscles were too tense to dismiss anything.

"There's no reason to hash all of this out now," Samuel concluded.

Leo disagreed. "Yeah, there is. There's no statute of limitations on murder, and if you drugged your wife, then it's murder."

Samuel froze. For a moment anyway. And he turned for the door. "If you have anything else to say to me, go through my lawyer."

"You're not leaving," Barrett warned him, stopping her father in his tracks. He glanced at Cybil. "Deputy Cassidy, why don't you wait here with Mr. Nash until his lawyer arrives? Then I'll start an interview."

Since Barrett had planned to interrogate him anyway, it didn't surprise Olivia that he'd want to go ahead and do that. But it clearly didn't please her father. Neither did the rest of what Barrett said.

"Leo, go ahead and contact the Texas Rangers about reopening the investigation into Simone's death. I'd like for them to get started on that ASAP in case it connects to what's going on now."

Her father stayed quiet for several moments, but he conveyed a lot with his glare, which had intensified. "You'll be sorry you ever started this," he said like a warning. A warning that he aimed at Olivia.

She didn't respond. Didn't have to. Leo saw to that. He picked up the laptops and motioned for her to follow him. She did. Not only because she wanted to put some distance between her father and herself but also because they were heading for the breakroom where she could check on Cameron. Olivia didn't even cast a glance at her dad, though she could practically feel him staring holes in her back.

"You okay?" Leo asked her.

No, she wasn't. She was shaken up by what'd just happened, but she wasn't going to dump that on him, too. He was already dealing with enough. Besides, he knew how hard that had been for her to face down a man who'd made an art form of bullying her.

And maybe an art form of murder, as well.

After all, it'd been years since her mother had died, and if he'd been responsible, then he'd been a free man all this time. Unpunished. But that could change. If that happened, if he did end up in jail for it, then she was just going to have to cope with the fact that she hadn't tried sooner to get justice for her mother.

Leo and she had just made it to the breakroom door when his phone rang again. He shifted the laptops in his arms so he could take it from his pocket. He hit the answer button and put the call on speaker.

"Well, I wish it'd been a hoax," Jace started the moment he was on the line, "but it wasn't. I found the body just up the road from Olivia's house. And yeah, the guy is definitely dead."

## Chapter Eleven

Leo had hoped that Jace was calling to tell them that all was well, but that hope vanished when he heard Jace's words.

A dead body.

Two in one day, and Leo figured it wasn't a co-incidence that Jace had found it so close to Olivia's house. No. This was connected to the attacks and the fires. Maybe even connected to her mother's death. Hell. It could be all one tangled mess with her father at the center.

"Who's dead?" Leo asked Jace.

"Not sure yet. That's because he's been shot in the face, and there's not much left of it."

Leo saw Olivia flinch, and he figured that had turned her stomach. It wasn't an easy image to have in your head.

"I've got my CSIs on the way out here," Jace went on, "and once they arrive and the scene is secured, I'll have a look around. There's no vehicle, no sign of a struggle in the immediate area. It looks like a body dump to me."

A body dump that was probably meant to be some kind of message to Olivia. A warning maybe or perhaps just a tool to torment her. But who was he and why had he been used as that warning/torment? Had he been a hired gun who'd screwed up enough that it'd cost him his life? If so, then Leo sure as hell wouldn't feel any sympathy for him. His only regret was that he wasn't alive so they could possibly get answers from him.

"I'll let you know when I've got an ID on the body," Jace said and ended the call.

Leo took a moment to gather his thoughts, looked at Olivia and figured she was going to need more than moment. He carried the laptops into the break-room and put them on the table. Did the same to the files she was carrying. Then he turned to her.

Yeah, she needed some time.

She certainly wouldn't want to go check on Cameron while her nerves were this frayed. Of course, there wasn't much he could do to help with that, but Leo still pulled her to him. Olivia came into his arms as if she belonged there. Leo didn't miss that, and apparently neither did she because the sound she made was part relief, part moan.

"I'm sorry," he told her because he didn't know what else to say.

It'd been a helluva morning what with being shot at, her house burned down, confronting her father and now this. Her life as she'd known it had vanished in a matter of a few hours. Added to that, they were about to take a step that could end up with Samuel being charged with murdering her mother. That would also mean he'd come darn close to getting Olivia killed, too.

"I'm trying to make sense of it," she said, her voice barely a whisper.

He was doing the same thing, but it wasn't adding up the way Leo wanted. He preferred it when all the pieces fit, and that wasn't happening.

Unless…

If Samuel had truly felt he was losing Olivia, he could have maybe set up her to take the fall for hiring Milton to kill Leo. Then Samuel could have petitioned for custody of Cameron, which Leo and Olivia had already considered. Considered, too, that everything after that could have been part of a plan that had just gotten away from him. Because, as much of a bullying snake as Samuel could be, Leo just couldn't see him endangering Cameron. It could be that this latest DB was a way of wrapping up a scheme that Samuel was trying to ditch.

"The danger could be over," Leo said, which had Olivia easing her head back to meet his eyes.

He saw her latch onto that hope, and it was a hope that he wished he could give her. Give *them*, he mentally corrected. But it was just a theory and they'd have to wait to see how it played out.

"Milton's in custody," he explained. "The second

gunman's dead, and since he had your mother's journals, it points to him being the one who set fire to your house. Maybe to Randall's truck, too."

Yet that was one of the puzzle pieces that didn't fit. Why Randall? Unless the person behind the attacks wanted to make Randall riled enough to come after Leo and kill him. Considering that possibility, Leo made a mental note to check on the man since Randall was scheduled to come in for an interview.

"You're thinking our attacker might just give up?" she asked.

*"Might,"* he said emphatically. "I still want us to take precautions, and I want this investigation to play out." He started to launch into some questions, but that could wait a couple more minutes. "Let's check on Cameron. If he's settled, then we can do some work."

She nodded but didn't move away. Leo didn't loosen his grip, either. They just stood there, both wearing their emotions on their sleeves. Not just the emotions of the dangers and threats but also the personal stuff.

He cursed. Groaned. "I don't know what the hell I'm going to do with you," he grumbled.

The corner of her mouth lifted into a half smile. "I feel the same way about you. We've been on opposites sides for so long that this feels wrong." She tipped her head into his arm that was around her. "And it feels right, too."

Leo totally got them. They couldn't just go back

and erase the nasty breakup or the way she'd shut him out of her life. But apparently the breakup and fallout afterward hadn't soured him on the notion that—yeah, it did feel right.

"Check on Cameron," he reminded her. Reminded himself, as well. And even then it still took several seconds for them to peel themselves away from each other and head to the bunkroom.

Izzie had put a quilt on the floor where both Cameron and she were sitting, his toys scattered around him. He was eating a snack, but he didn't seem especially happy about it.

"He's still so tired that I'm going to try to get him to finish out his nap after he eats," Izzie explained.

"You need me to help?" Olivia asked.

Izzie shook her head. "I can manage." She paused. "How's everything going?"

Leo didn't want to fill her in on the dead bodies with Cameron around so he settled for saying, "There have been some new developments in the case. As soon as the bomb squad's done at my house, though, we should be able to go back."

The nanny seemed to understand that "going back" might not happen for a while. "All right. Then, let me get this boy to sleep."

Olivia and Leo gave Cameron a quick kiss and left them to go back to the breakroom. The first thing Leo did was point to the fridge. "There'll be Cokes, water and maybe even some snacks in there. Help yourself."

Leo settled for a cup of coffee. While he was pouring it, he called a friend, Texas Ranger Griff Morris. The call went to voice mail so Leo left him a message, explaining that some new concerns and questions had resurfaced in the fatal car accident of Simone Nash and that he wanted Griff to use some leverage to have the case reopened. Leo had no doubts that Griff would make it happen.

When he turned back around, he saw that Olivia was staring at him. "A problem?" he asked.

She quickly shook her head. "I, uh, it's hard to explain." She paused and eased into the chair as if her legs had given way. "It's just…if my father is guilty, then it'll be hard. In some way, it'll be like losing her all over again."

He understood that and hated this was something Olivia would have to go through. "Do you still have nightmares about the accident?" Because he recalled her having a bad one when they'd been lovers and she'd stay the night at his place.

"Sometimes." She shook her head again, but this time he thought she was trying to push aside the images. Ones that didn't wait until nightmares to surface. "That's why the reopened investigation will be hard. The Rangers will have to question me, and I'll have to go through it in detail."

Leo frowned. "You'd rather keep this as is?"

"No," Olivia quickly answered. "No," she repeated on a heavy sigh. "If my father killed her, then he needs to answer for that. And my reliving it will be just a price I have to pay for making sure he doesn't get away with it."

Reliving it wouldn't be easy, and Leo wasn't sure he could help her with that. He'd try, though. Especially since it was his attack that had brought all of this back to the surface.

He slid his hand over hers and cursed himself because he was going to have to bring even more to the surface. "I know Barrett asked you if there was anything in the journals that connect to the attacks…" he reminded her. "You said no, but is there a chance there's really something in your mother's journals to incriminate your father?"

Olivia drew in a long breath and then released it before she spoke. "Nothing that I can think of. I've read every entry multiple times," she added.

"What about your father?" Leo asked. "Has he read them?"

"I'm not positive, but I don't think he did. My mother didn't keep them in plain sight, and I'd never heard my father mention them before today."

Leo gave that some thought. "She didn't keep them in plain sight, but Bernice could have snooped around, found them and showed them to your father. Any reason she'd do something like that?"

"Oh, Bernice would do it. She's always been fiercely loyal to my dad. I knew that even when I was ten years old. So, yes, Bernice could have found them and showed them to him if she thought my dad would *appreciate* her doing it."

"'Appreciate'?" Leo repeated. "Nothing sexual between them, though?"

"No. I'm sure of that. There's a different vibe when he's with Bernice than there is when he brings his other women around. Like with Rena, for instance."

Leo paused again. "Could Rena have known about the journals? How soon did she start seeing your dad after your mom's death."

Her mouth tightened. "Rena's been around a long time, and yes, maybe he was with her while my mom was still alive. Rena and he used to do charity fundraiser stuff together. As for the journals, maybe Rena would know, but if she did, she wouldn't have learned about it from my mother."

"Your mom didn't like Rena?" he asked, obviously considering that.

"I don't think so. I remember Rena's name coming up in a couple of their arguments."

Interesting. So, maybe Rena could have egged Samuel on to kill his wife. Then again, Rena could have done it.

"Do you remember if Rena was around the estate about the time of your mother's car accident?" he asked.

"No." She stopped, her eyes widening. "Oh, I see. You believe Rena could have given my mom those drugs?"

"Do you believe it?" he countered.

She took another of those deep breaths, but this

one had a weariness to it. And Leo knew why. Her mother's case hadn't even been officially reopened, and here Olivia was having to pull all these memories back to the surface. To the surface where they could take little bites out of her all over again.

"I don't know if Rena could have done it," she finally answered. "Sometimes, I think she's as obsessed with my father as Bernice, just in a different kind of way."

Yeah, Leo was coming to the same conclusion. Both women had their own way of being toxic. Then again, Samuel was a toxic kind of guy himself, so he deserved them both.

He hated to keep digging at Olivia, but Leo couldn't get past the look on Samuel's face when he'd seen the journals in the evidence bag. "Your father didn't know you'd kept the journals. I'm guessing that means you didn't show them to him over the years?"

"No," she readily answered. "My mom always said they were secrets that she shared only with me. So, a couple of weeks after her death, after I got out of the hospital, I went into her office and got them because I heard Bernice say they were going to clean out the room. I didn't want them getting tossed. Or read," she added. "I wanted to keep her secrets."

"So you hid them," Leo concluded, and he waited for her to confirm that with a nod. "But your father did recognize them, so he must have seen them at one point?"

Again, she gave him a confirming nod. "I can't say, though, when that happened. My mother wrote in them for years, so there would have been countless opportunities for him to see them."

Definitely. And countless opportunities for Samuel to object to what his wife had put in those entries. "Your mother wrote about the arguments and such that she had with your dad?"

"She did a couple of times. You can read the entries for yourself," Olivia offered. "When I was in high school, I scanned the pages and put them in an online storage cloud. That way, if anything happened to the journals, I'd still have what my mother had written."

Though Leo figured it'd take more time than he had to go through years of her mom's journal entries, he knew it was something that had to be done. He'd need to read them with an objective eye, a cop's eye, to see if there was anything that Olivia had missed. Of course, that likely meant Olivia would be rereading them, which wouldn't help her tamp down those memories that still gave her nightmares.

"Download them," he instructed and gave her hand a gentle squeeze. He knew it was a lame gesture considering what this would end up costing her. But apparently Olivia didn't consider it so lame because she smiled at him.

Oh man.

A smile wasn't good. Not now anyway. It made him want to taste that smile. Taste the rest of her, too. Thankfully, he didn't have to dig up enough willpower to resist her because his phone rang and he saw a familiar name on the screen. Morgan Strait, the head of the bomb squad unit that'd been at his place.

"Morgan," Leo greeted when he answered the call. "You have good news for me?"

"I do," the man assured him. "We've gone through every inch of your house and the grounds surrounding it, and we haven't found a thing."

Leo felt some of the tightness in his chest ease up a little.

"I still have men working their way through your barns and outbuildings," Morgan went on, "but none of those are close enough to your house to do any damage if there happened to be an incendiary device in any of them. I've instructed your hands to stay away from them just in case."

"That is good news," Leo told him.

"The bad news is that I don't have the manpower to go through every acre of your ranch, so someone could have rigged something on the trails or the pastures. Heck, even in the shrubs or trees. My advice would be to have your hands be on the lookout for anything suspicious."

"Thanks. I will."

"No problem," Morgan said. "We'll be wrapping up here in about an hour if you want to come back."

Leo very much wanted to do that. The sheriff's office was safe, but Cameron, Izzie and Olivia would be much more comfortable at his place than here. Of course, that'd mean not having the hands check the pastures since Leo would want them close to the house.

"What about Randall's truck?" Leo asked. "Have you had a chance to look at it?"

"I did, and there was definitely something used to trigger the explosion. Not sure what yet. The lab will need to look at it, but they should be able to tell us something. In the meantime, I'm having what's left of the truck towed to a large evidence holding facility in San Antonio. Have the owner contact me if he has any questions about when and if he can get back his property."

"I will." Though so far Leo hadn't had any luck getting in touch with Randall. Still, when the man surfaced, he'd probably want answers, not only about the truck but maybe about everything else, as well.

Leo thanked Morgan again and turned back to relay what he'd just learned to Olivia.

"You can go home," she said, letting him know that she'd gotten the gist of the conversation.

He nodded, would have added more, but he heard a loud voice coming from the front of the building. Leo couldn't make out the exact words, but the tone was definitely one of anger. And that anger was coming from none other than Samuel.

Olivia sighed, got to her feet. "I can see what he's yelling about," she offered.

But Leo had no intention of sending her out. Not when Samuel was at the top of their suspect list. With Olivia right on his heels, he hurried from the breakroom to see if Barrett or Cybil needed any assistance.

"I didn't try to kill anyone," Samuel was shouting. "Not my wife. Not your brother." He'd added his usual venom to the *your brother*, and Leo knew that part was for him.

Rena was there, as well. She was behind Samuel, had hold of both of his arms and was a doing a fairly decent job of keeping him from charging at Barrett and Cybil. That would have been a Texas-sized mistake because not only were Barrett and the deputy armed, Barrett could have taken down the man with a single punch.

Samuel immediately shifted his attention to Leo and Olivia, and Leo hadn't thought it possible, but the man's scowl was even worse than what it had been earlier.

"The sheriff just read me my rights," Samuel roared. He stopped struggling, but Rena kept her arms wrapped tightly around him.

"Because he wouldn't shut up," Barrett explained. "I figured if he kept yakking, he might blurt something out, something I couldn't use against him if I didn't Mirandize him first."

So, apparently Samuel hadn't waited for his attorney, and it was also obvious that he wasn't going to heed his right to remain silent.

"I won't be treated like this," Samuel snarled. "I won't let my daughter taint my name with nonsense allegations that I killed her mother. Those journals mean nothing. Nothing! And they shouldn't have any part in this."

He hadn't said *my daughter* with any affection whatsoever. Just the opposite. Olivia was his enemy now, too. Apparently, so were those journals.

"Calm down, Samuel," Rena insisted, her voice a lot calmer and softer than his. The woman was practically cooing to him. "Your blood pressure's probably through the roof right now. Come with me and let's talk. I can get you some water."

Samuel put up some resistance. At first. But after a couple of seconds where he glared at Olivia, the man allowed Rena to lead him to the other side of the room where there was a water cooler. She did, indeed, get him a drink and then practically sandwiched him against the wall while she continued to talk to him in a murmur.

Cybil waited for the nod from Barrett. When she got it, the deputy went back to the dispatch desk. Barrett stayed next to Olivia and Leo, not exactly in a huddle but close, and all three of them cast wary glances at Samuel.

"Olivia's downloading the pages of her mother's journal." Leo kept his voice low when he spoke to his brother. "After hearing Samuel's latest outburst, I'm even more interested in reading them."

Barrett made a sound of agreement. "Samuel's definitely worried about them."

As if to prove that, Leo saw Samuel's eyes drift into Barrett's office. He was pretty sure the man was looking at the evidence bag of journals on Barrett's desk. Rena followed his gaze and then saw, too, that Barrett, Olivia and Leo were watching them. She caught Samuel's chin, turning him back to face her. Leo couldn't hear what the woman said to him, but Samuel seemed to be listening.

Leo thought about Rena's claim that Samuel and she would get back together. It certainly seemed as if that was exactly what was happening.

Olivia sighed, causing Leo to turn to her. He was pretty sure they were on the same page of thought when it came to Rena and Samuel. The easy intimacy between them had Leo considering if maybe they had worked together to stage the attacks and set up Simone's car accident. But that didn't feel right because, if that's what had indeed happened, then Leo couldn't see Rena keeping that to herself when Samuel and she were on the outs. A woman capable of writing those threatening emails didn't stay silent about much.

"I told Leo that I thought my father was more agitated than usual about my mother because the anniversary of her death is coming up," Olivia explained. She stopped and shook her head. "But maybe it's more than that. Maybe it's guilt."

Neither Barrett nor Leo disputed that, and Leo watched again as Samuel glanced over at the journals.

"He thinks Simone wrote something incriminating," Leo concluded. "He's worried about what we'll find when we read them."

Barrett made a sound of agreement.

"I wish there was something incriminating to find," Olivia said, punctuated with another of those sighs. "I wish there was something in them that would make him come clean about what happened, because I believe there could be more to it than what he's admitted."

Leo thought that, as well. That's why he considered something. It was a long shot. More of a weak bluff. But sometimes all it took was a nudge, and maybe this would be the right one.

"What if you tell your father that there is something?" Leo suggested, still whispering. "What if you lie and say that your mother wrote that someone was trying to kill her?"

Leo figured it would take Olivia a couple of minutes to mull that over. She didn't. She nodded and immediately moved away from Barrett and him. Walking closer to her father, she pointed to the journals.

"You're worried about what's in those," Olivia

said, her voice surprisingly strong. "Well, you should be."

It wasn't anger now that flashed in Samuel's eyes but rather concern. Maybe even fear. Rena didn't have as extreme of a reaction, but she definitely quit cooing and soothing.

"What do you mean?" Rena asked. "Did Simone say something...bad?"

"Yes," Olivia said, adding to the lie. "She said someone was trying to kill her." And with that, she stared directly at her father.

Leo steeled himself for the burst of outrage he figured they were about to get from Samuel. But no outburst. The man just wearily shook his head and squeezed his eyes shut. Then he said a single word that Leo definitely hadn't been expecting.

"Bernice," Samuel muttered, still shaking his head. "Bernice wanted Simone dead."

## Chapter Twelve

When Olivia had decided to go with the impromptu ruse to get her father to say something incriminating, she hadn't actually expected it to work. Nor had she thought that name would come out of his mouth.

"Bernice?" Olivia repeated.

Both Barrett and Leo moved closer, flanking her, while the three of them faced down her father. Their stares were definitely demands for him to explain why he'd just blurted out Bernice's name.

Samuel cursed, pushed the cup of water away that Rena was offering him, and he began to pace. "I shouldn't have said that," he grumbled. "I don't have any proof that Bernice did anything wrong."

He was backpedaling, which wouldn't help them get to the truth.

"But you must suspect her," Olivia quickly pointed out. "Did Bernice give my mother those drugs the night of the car wreck? Did she?" Olivia pressed when her father didn't answer. She finally stepped in front of him, stopping him and facing him down. "Did she?"

Her father looked at the spot just above her shoulder. Definitely avoiding eye contact. "Maybe," he finally said.

"She's certainly capable of that," Rena insisted. "The woman is a control freak. She probably wanted your mother out of the way so she'd have a better shot at getting more of Samuel's attention."

Samuel sniped Rena a scowl. "If Bernice did it, it wasn't because she wanted Simone out of the way," he snapped.

"Then why?" Olivia demanded.

Her father groaned and tried to pace again, but Olivia did another block, pinning him between Rena on one side and Barrett and Leo on the other.

"Bernice thought Simone was no longer thinking clearly," her father said, and it sounded to Olivia as if he were carefully choosing his words. "Bernice believed, wrongfully so, that Simone would leave—disappear," he amended, "and that Simone would take you with her so I'd never be able to see you again. Bernice knew that'd crush me."

Olivia tried to pick through that to see if she could tell if he was lying. She just didn't know. But it didn't surprise her that Bernice would have such a strong opinion of her mother or that her father's household manager would be privy to her parents' marital problems. The truth was Simone had spoken of a divorce, so it wouldn't be much of a stretch for Bernice to believe that Simone would take her daughter with her when she left the estate.

"I want you to go through every detail of what happened that night," Barrett told her father as he took out his phone. "I'll call Bernice and get her back in here. I'll need to hear what she has to say about all this."

Her father cursed again, and Olivia could see that he regretted opening the subject. But it could lead to something. A confession, maybe. Then again, even if Bernice had had something to do with her mother's death, it wouldn't clear up the recent attacks and fires.

Barrett stepped into his office to make the call, and Olivia continued to stare at her father. "Why didn't you say anything about Bernice before now?" she demanded when he didn't continue.

"Because I don't know if my suspicions are right." He dragged his hand over his face. "What I do know is your mother didn't use drugs, period. So, either she dosed herself up that night for the first time, or someone else did it. I didn't do it, so that leaves Bernice."

Maybe, but Olivia shifted her attention to the woman who was now patting her father's arm. "Were you at the estate that night?" Olivia asked her.

Rena's eyes widened and her mouth dropped open. "You're accusing me now?" she shrieked.

"*Asking* you," Leo clarified. "But I'm going to insist that you answer the question."

Rena's indignance meshed with the anger. "No, I wasn't there. If I remember correctly, your father and I had some business a week or so before that, but I wasn't in the house when Simone died."

Both Leo and Olivia looked to her father to confirm what Rena had just said, but he only shrugged. "I don't remember a lot about that night," he admitted. "Simone and I argued, and she stormed out. She said she was going out for a drive. After she left, I had a few drinks. Maybe more than a few," he added in a mumble.

"Was Simone acting as if she'd been drugged while you two were arguing?" Leo pressed.

Her father stayed quiet a moment and his forehead bunched up as if he were trying hard to pull out the memories. Or else that's what he wanted them to think. But it could be an act. All of this could be an act.

"No," her father finally said. "Not drunk or high. She was just pissed off." He paused again. "But she didn't leave right away after she stormed out. I think it was at least a half hour before she left."

"At least a half hour," Olivia agreed.

And here it came. Her own flood of memories. She didn't know how they could manage to stay so fresh, so raw, after all this time. Her father's recollections didn't include the wreck itself. Nor had he heard the sound of her mother's dying breath.

Leo turned to her. "Are you okay?" he whispered.

Olivia nodded and, even though the nod was a lie,

she pushed the images and the sounds aside so she could explain her version of the timing of that night.

"I heard the argument between my parents," she said. "I heard my mom say she was going to leave, so I sneaked into the garage and got into her car. I didn't have a watch, but I know she didn't come out in only a few minutes. It was much longer than that. In fact, I'd fallen asleep."

Olivia had no idea how long it'd been before the drugs in her mother's system had taken effect, but that was something she intended to find out.

"Bernice will be here in a couple of minutes," Barrett announced when he returned from making his call. "She's at the diner just up the street."

It surprised Olivia that Bernice hadn't gone back to the estate. Then again, the woman might not have wanted to make that trip since Barrett had made it clear earlier that he wanted to interview her. Now, he'd have something else to question her about.

Her possible involvement in Simone's death.

Olivia didn't have to guess how Bernice would react to that. She would be many steps past being enraged, and the woman was likely to aim that rage at Samuel. After all, he'd been the one to throw Bernice's name into the mix of suspects.

Leo's phone rang, and he showed her the screen after he checked it. Jace. That meant this could be important.

"We can take this in Barrett's office," Leo told her, and Olivia headed there with him.

Obviously, Leo hadn't wanted to have this conversation in front of her father and Rena, and he shut the door before he put the call on speaker.

"I got an ID on the body," Jace said, not starting with a greeting. "And it's someone you know. Randall Arnett."

Leo jerked back his head. No doubt in surprise. Olivia was having a similar reaction and because her legs suddenly felt a little unsteady, she caught onto the edge of Barrett's desk.

"You're sure it's Randall?" Leo asked, taking the question right out of her mouth. After all, the body that Jace had found had been shot in the face, which would make it hard to ID him. Olivia couldn't help but wonder if Randall had set up his own death.

"Yeah," Jace verified. "I did a quick fingerprint check and I got a hit. It's Randall, all right."

So, not a faked death. Probably not suicide, either, because she remembered Jace saying it'd looked like a body dump.

"He can't have been dead for long," Leo said. "His truck blew up at my place just a couple of hours ago. He was injured, but he was still able to run off."

"Why'd he run?" Jace wanted to know.

"He said something about me trying to kill him. I guess he thought I'd put the firebomb in his truck." Leo stopped. "But I don't know why he drove to my place to tell me that. And I sure as hell don't know how he got from my ranch to Olivia's."

She was trying to figure out the same thing. Her

house wasn't far from Leo's, but it would have taken Randall hours and hours had he been traveling on foot. Plus, on foot wouldn't mesh with Jace's body dump theory.

"So someone gave Randall a ride," Olivia concluded.

"Or else he went back to his ranch and got another vehicle," Leo suggested.

True. A trip like that wouldn't have taken nearly as long as getting to her place. "Did you find another vehicle near Randall's body?" she asked.

"No. But I did find a phone, and I'm taking it into evidence. Maybe it belongs to the killer. Or if it's Randall's, he could have called the person who ended up killing him." Jace muttered some profanity that had a frustrated edge to it. "Or the phone could belong to one of the responders to the fire. I'll let you know when I figure it out."

Leo thanked him, ended the call and glanced back toward the squad room where they'd left her father and Rena. He dragged in a deep breath as if steeling himself for another round, but he didn't move. Neither did she because she, too, needed a moment to compose herself.

"Since I believe Randall got away with murdering his girlfriend," she said, "it's hard for me to feel sympathy for him. Still…" She left it at that.

Leo's nod let her know that his feelings were leaning the same way. Randall's murder now made him a victim. A victim almost certainly connected to the attacks on Leo and her. Why else would his body have been left so close to her house? Even if the reason was just to muddy the investigation, it was still another body to add to the death toll.

A toll that the killer would no doubt like to add to by murdering both Leo and Olivia.

"This takes Randall off the suspect list," she muttered, talking more to herself than to Leo.

But Leo made a sound of agreement. "That doesn't mean, though, that he didn't set up the attacks."

Her mind took a mental stutter and she shook her head. Olivia was about to say that didn't seem possible, but then she considered it from a different angle.

"You think Randall's own hired gun could have killed him?" she asked.

"It's possible. Maybe the hired gun got spooked when his comrade, Lowell, was killed. Or Randall could have reneged on payment or done something else to make this guy off him. Killers aren't known for playing by the rules."

No, they weren't, and this could certainly have been a plan that'd backfired on Randall.

"Milton," Leo added a moment later. "He might be willing to talk now when we tell him about Lowell's and Randall's murders. It could make him scared enough to finally rat on who hired him."

Yes, Olivia could see that happening and, if so, Leo might have been right about the danger finally being over.

Leo ran his hand down her arm. "I have to go out

there and help Barrett deal with this mess. You can go back to the breakroom if you want."

It was tempting. Mercy, was it. She was drained and shaky, and Olivia doubted being around her father and Rena would improve that. Still, she couldn't just put her head in the sand, especially since one of them might say something that would help shed some light on her mother's fatal car wreck and the current investigation.

The sound of a bell ringing had them both moving. Because it was the bell on the front door and it meant someone had come in. Olivia didn't have to guess who that someone was because she immediately heard Rena say Bernice's name.

Leo and Olivia entered the squad room, but before they dealt with Bernice, Leo pulled his brother aside and whispered, "The DB at Olivia's is Randall's."

Barrett got the same shocked expression that Leo and she had had. "I'll want details about that later," he said on a sigh just as Rena blurted something to Bernice.

"Samuel thinks you killed Simone."

Olivia turned in time to catch Bernice's reaction. If looks could kill, Bernice would have certainly accomplished it with the stony glare she aimed at Rena.

"What are you blathering about now?" Bernice asked.

"Rena," her father warned, taking hold of her arm.

But Rena just shook off his grip and went closer to Bernice. "Samuel thinks you might have killed

Simone," Rena repeated. There was a smugness to her tone and expression, probably because she'd waited for years to have Samuel put Bernice in her place.

But this was more than "her place." This was an accusation that could land Bernice in jail for the rest of her life.

Bernice shifted her attention to Samuel. "What's she talking about?"

His head dropped down for a moment and then, on a heavy sigh, he stepped closer to Bernice. "I know you didn't like Simone," he said.

That was it. Apparently, the full explanation he intended to give her. But it was enough. Olivia saw the verbal blow land on Bernice as effectively as a heavyweight's fist. The woman flinched, and there was no longer anger in her eyes. Just the unbearable hurt of betrayal by someone she almost certainly loved.

The shock didn't last long, though. She pressed her lips together for a moment, cleared her throat and turned to Olivia.

"You told your father that I might have killed your mother?" Bernice asked. There was a coldness now; a thick layer of ice far more formidable than anger.

Olivia ignored the question and went with one of her own. "Did you kill her?"

Bernice looked her straight in the eyes. "No. It's true that I didn't like her, but I didn't have anything to do with her death." She turned, aiming that cold at Samuel now. "But you believe I did?"

He didn't break eye contact with Bernice, either.

"I believe it's possible that you could have been trying to protect me by getting Simone out of the way."

Again, that was a blow, and this time Bernice's icy facade shattered a little. The sound she made was a hollow laugh. This time, it took several more moments for her to compose herself. And just like that, the anger was back. Anger she aimed not at Samuel but at Rena.

"I don't have to guess that you put all of this nonsense into Samuel's head," Bernice said, not waiting for the woman to respond. "Did you also remind him that you had a much stronger motive than I did for *getting Simone out of the way*?" She added some extra bite to those last words.

In contrast, Rena looked completely unruffled. "I had no motive. Simone and Samuel's marriage was falling apart. It was only a matter of time before they got a divorce. There was no reason for me to hurry that along."

"No reason other than the biggest one of all," Bernice argued. "You could have killed her so you could get your claws into Samuel sooner. No waiting for a divorce. But that didn't work, did it? Here it is, all these years later, and you still don't have Samuel."

That caused Rena's *unruffled* to shatter and she hooked her arm possessively through Samuel's. "You jealous witch. You're the one who's tried to get her claws into him—"

"Stop!" Barrett snapped, issuing his cop's glare

at Rena, Bernice and her father before looking at his deputy. "Go ahead, Deputy Cassidy, and take Bernice to an interview room so we can get her statement on record. I'll need the same from both of you," he added to Samuel and Rena.

That didn't please any of the three. They turned their displeasured looks to Barrett, which he ignored. He motioned for Cybil to go ahead and take Bernice out of there.

But Bernice held her ground. "Did Rena tell you that she was at the estate a lot in those days before Simone's death?"

"I wasn't," Rena insisted. "It'd been at least a week."

"I keep very good records," Bernice said, and it sounded like a threat. "You were there nearly every day the week she died. And I suspect you're the one who drugged her."

"What!" Rena howled in outrage.

"I think you put the drugs in Simone's tea or maybe that energy juice she was always drinking. Maybe you got lucky with the timing of her getting behind the wheel, or maybe you just thought she'd die of a drug overdose. Either way, I'm sure the sheriff will take a hard look at you."

"Oh, I will," Barrett assured her and gestured again for Cybil to take Bernice away. This time, Bernice cooperated but not before she shot Samuel one final glare.

Her father muttered some curse words that

seemed to be aimed at himself. Perhaps because he hadn't wanted things to play out like this.

That seemed to be Rena's take on things anyway.

"Don't you dare feel sorry for that woman," Rena snapped. "You should have fired her years ago. She's done nothing but run your life, and she's done that by trying to shut me out."

That put some strength in her father's spine and he pulled back his shoulders while staring at Rena. "Don't you dare try to make this about you." He turned to Barrett. "I'd like to wait in an interview room, too, while I call my lawyer."

Barrett nodded and motioned to the hall. "Just go that way and take the room that isn't occupied by Bernice."

"It is about me," Rena called out to him. "It's about Bernice turning you against me any chance she gets."

Apparently, Rena couldn't see that she was trying to do the same thing to Bernice. Olivia found the two exhausting and wasn't surprised when her father walked away, turning his back on Rena.

Tears filled Rena's eyes, but that didn't stop her from giving one of the desk chairs an angry kick.

"You wait there," Barrett warned her and motioned toward the chairs in front of the dispatch desk. "If you leave, I'll charge you with obstruction."

That didn't improve Rena's mood, and she whipped out her phone, saying she was calling her lawyer. Barrett left her to that and tipped his head for Leo and Olivia to follow him into his office.

"Tell me what happened to Randall," Barrett said the moment he had his office door closed.

"Jace and I both got a call about an hour ago to tell us about a body near Olivia's," Leo explained. "Jace checked it out and found Randall. He'd been shot in the face, but Jace ID'd him through fingerprints."

Obviously processing the information, Barrett sat on the edge of his desk. "About an hour ago," he repeated. "Shortly after the time Olivia and you got back here to the sheriff's office."

"Yeah," Leo said, and it seemed to Olivia as if he was also agreeing with something else his brother hadn't spelled out. "It means Rena, Samuel or Bernice could have gotten to Randall, killed him and dumped the body."

"The question is—why?" Barrett continued. "Other than to distract us or to throw a wrench in the investigation, I can't see why. Unless—"

"Randall's connected to the attacks or the hired thugs used in the attacks," Leo finished for him.

Barrett nodded and took out his phone. "I'll text Cybil and have her ask Samuel about an alibi. He probably won't want to say anything without his lawyer, but he might slip up. I also need to call the diner. I want to see how long Bernice was there before I had her come back here."

Olivia considered herself a step behind the two lawmen when it came to following the threads of this investigation, but she latched onto this angle right away. The person who'd killed Randall had called both Leo and Jace. Had maybe even personally done the body dump. Bernice couldn't have managed that if she'd been sitting in the town's diner for the past couple of hours.

While Barrett made the call, Olivia glanced out at Rena, to make sure she was still there. She was. And the woman was still on the phone, maybe griping to her lawyer.

Or plotting another attack.

"Don't worry," Leo said. "We'll check her alibi, too."

Rena would probably claim she wasn't capable of killing Randall and shoving him out of a vehicle. And maybe she wasn't. But Rena worked out a lot. In fact, of their three remaining suspects—Rena, Bernice and Olivia's father—Olivia thought Rena might be the strongest of them physically. Of course, it wouldn't have taken strength had the person responsible hired some muscle to do their dirty work.

"Bernice had only been at the diner for about ten minutes when I called her," Barrett relayed when he got off the phone.

So, no alibi. Well, not one in the diner anyway. That didn't mean the woman couldn't account for where she was and what she was doing. Barrett would certainly try to get the info out of her.

"I have another possible angle," Leo said, making his own call. He held up a finger in a wait-a-second gesture when Barrett questioned him. The person he'd called had obviously answered. "Jace," Leo greeted, putting the call on speaker. "Anything on that phone you found near Randall's body?"

"No. I haven't gotten into it yet. It's got a passcode, so I'll have to see if the lab can do anything with it."

Leo groaned. "That could take days," he mumbled to her. "Weeks even."

Olivia wanted to groan, too. They didn't have that kind of time. Heck, they might not even have hours before someone tried to attack them again.

"But I was about to call you about something else," Jace continued a moment later. "I've got an eyewitness in Olivia's neighborhood who saw a black SUV around the time the body would have been dumped. It's a woman who lives across the street, and she said she's seen that vehicle or one like it many times before. She said she couldn't see inside because the windows are tinted."

That got Olivia's attention. "What vehicle?" she asked.

"One with a logo on the driver's-side door."

And suddenly Olivia knew exactly what logo Jace meant. "A sycamore leaf?" she managed to ask.

"Yeah," Jace verified. "I was just checking, and the only vehicles anyone around here has seen like that all belong to your father."

## Chapter Thirteen

What he was doing was a risk, but Leo knew anything he did at this point would be. Still, it'd bring some normalcy back to Cameron's life. Or at least it would if Leo could get his son, Olivia and Izzie safely back to the ranch.

The fire department and bomb squad had given Leo the all-clear to return, so at least he didn't have to worry about the specific threat of the place going up in flames. And he'd added even more security, bringing over some ranch hands from Barrett's place to patrol the grounds and prevent someone from sneaking onto the property and putting some sniper skills to bad use.

Still…

Yeah, that *still* was going to haunt him until he had everyone tucked safely inside the house.

Izzie was treating the ride in the cruiser as a fun adventure for Cameron by reading to him from a book that made animal sounds whenever Cameron touched one of the pages. His son was giggling, definitely not showing any signs of worry or fear. Unlike Olivia and Leo.

Olivia was keeping watch as he drove to the ranch. Leo was, as well, and so were Cybil and Daniel, who were in the cruiser behind them. Unfortunately, his fellow deputy and brother wouldn't be able to stay at the ranch. There was just too much going on at the sheriff's office, and that's where Leo needed them to be. Their best chance at ending the danger was to get answers from their now three suspects and to follow the new lead they'd gotten from Jace.

Someone had used one of the vehicles from the Sycamore Grove estate, and Leo wanted to know which who. If Barrett couldn't pull that info out of Rena, Bernice and Samuel, then maybe he'd be able to hold them for at least a couple of hours.

Until Leo could make this drive and get off the roads.

As long as they were out in the open, the risks skyrocketed. It would have been worse, though, to make the trip at night. That's why Leo had timed it so that it was still a while before sunset.

He held his breath when he took the turn to his ranch and then released that breath when he realized someone had already removed Randall's truck from the road. Good. That was one of the reasons Leo hadn't left the sheriff's office any sooner and had in fact stayed nearly eight hours after getting the call from Jace.

Along with setting up those extra security measures, Leo had wanted to give the bomb squad time to deal with the truck. If not, he would have had to use the trails to get to his house, and he hadn't wanted to risk driving them since they would be prime areas for another sniper to lay in wait.

He drove past the burned-out area left by Randall's truck and spotted the first of the hands. There were others, all armed and clearly on guard, just as Leo had instructed. Another was on the porch where he would stay until Leo had Olivia, Izzie and Cameron inside. Then he would join the other hands to patrol the ranch. If a gunman managed to get past the ranch hands, then Leo would have the security system turned on to alert them if anyone tried to break in.

Leo parked the cruiser in the garage and quickly got Cameron into the house. Olivia and Izzie were right on his heels, and the moment he'd reset the security system, he fired off a quick text to Daniel and Cybil to let them know it was okay for them to go back to town.

"I can take Cameron to the nursery," Izzie volunteered, easing Cameron into her arms and looping the diaper bag over her shoulder. "I'm sure he needs to be changed. Then I'll bathe him and get him ready for bed. I'll let you know before I put him down so you can say good-night to him."

Leo was thankful the nanny was there to keep Cameron on schedule. Doing that was huge, and it freed him up to try to make some headway on the investigation.

"I can sleep in the nursery with Cameron, if that's okay," Izzie offered.

Leo thought that staying with his son was something he'd like to do. The trouble was, he wasn't sure when Olivia and he would be turning in for the night, and Izzie probably didn't want to stay in limbo, waiting for them to decide. He nodded, thanked her, but knew that he'd be sleeping very close to his boy. No way did he want to be too far away from Cameron in case something went wrong.

When Izzie left with Cameron, Leo turned to Olivia to see how she was holding up. As if she knew he was checking for that, she lifted her chin and put on what he thought was a decent attempt at a strong expression. But he knew beneath the surface that she was just as rattled as he was. Heck, they were all rattled, including his brothers, which was a reminder for him to get in touch with Barrett to let him know that they'd arrived safely.

He took out his phone and pressed Barrett's number. He answered on the first ring. "We're home," Leo told him. "We're okay."

"Good. I didn't want to call you while you were on the road. Didn't figure you'd want the distraction."

"If it's good news, it's not a distraction," Leo quickly assured him.

"Sorry. It's not good. Bernice, Rena and Samuel have all lawyered up. The three of them did insist, though, that they're innocent, but since none of them is spouting proof of an alibi, I'm guessing they don't have any."

So, they wouldn't be able to eliminate any one of them. Not yet. But now that Bernice wasn't so chummy with Samuel, the woman might be willing to spill some secrets about him. Samuel might be willing to do the same.

Leo ended the call with Barrett and turned back to Olivia. Even though he hadn't put the call on speaker, she'd obviously heard, and she sighed.

"Hiding behind their lawyers," she muttered. "I guess it was too much to expect for one of them to confess."

Yes, it was. A confession now would result in charges for first-degree murder, attempted murder, assault with a deadly weapon, and conspiracy. If convicted, the death penalty would be on the table. Plus, Leo doubted that any of the three had their consciences troubling them enough to come clean.

"I'm sure you didn't get much sleep last night," he said after she made another weary sigh. She looked exhausted and no doubt felt it, too. "You should probably try to rest at least for a little while. There's a bed in the guest room or you could go into my room."

Olivia lifted an eyebrow, and he realized that his suggestion had sounded a little like a come-on. Probably because they'd had sex in his room and it'd been damn amazing.

"You're too tired for sex," he added.

He'd tried to go for light, but he'd failed big-time. Her eyebrow quirked again, and she stepped into his arms, sliding her hands around him until they were body to body. Until breath met breath.

Suddenly, he didn't feel too tired or too busy for sex. But it couldn't happen. Not when their little boy could still be in danger.

Leo settled for brushing his mouth over her cheek. It was the kind of kiss meant to soothe. And maybe it had. But the rest of his stupid body reminded him that it was only a short distance from her cheek to her mouth. Of course, a real kiss would break some rules and only make him want more. *More* couldn't happen. Not right now anyway. But it would be night soon, and eventually they'd have to go to bed.

Maybe even go to bed together.

Sex did seem inevitable between them. It didn't seem to matter how much they fought it, how much they knew it shouldn't happen.

And that's why Leo broke one of those rules and kissed her.

Since the kiss was a huge mistake and couldn't last long, he made it count. He deepened it, letting the taste of Olivia slide right through him. The heat was right behind the taste. Then the need. Of course, the need had never been far from the surface when it came to the two of them.

As the heat urged him to kick things up even more, Leo pulled away from her. Her breath was gusting. Her face flushed. And her mouth looked as if it'd just been thoroughly kissed.

"I'm glad you weren't too tired for that," she

murmured in a voice that was as effective as a siren's lure.

So was he. But now he had to do something to get rid of the cloud the kiss had put in his mind. It took some doing to focus on something other than Olivia.

"I need to go through your mother's journals," he said, and he watched as that shifted her back to reality.

No gusting breath or flushed face for her now. Just a resigned nod. "Barrett copied everything that was in the envelope Bernice gave him," she said. "I can look through that while you're on the journals."

It seemed like a good way to divide the work. Then, if neither of them hit on anything new, they could trade stashes. Leo also needed to make time to get warrants to go through the financials for all of their suspects. With the eyewitness account of the vehicle that'd been at Olivia's, that might be enough to convince a judge to let him take a look at bank accounts to see if anyone had recently paid for a hitman or two.

Leo picked up the bag with the laptops and files he'd brought from the sheriff's office. "We can set up in the room next to the nursery," he suggested. "That way, we can keep an eye on Cameron."

Olivia readily agreed and didn't say a word about a bed being in there. That made her a wise woman since there was no need to add any more sexual fuel to this attraction.

Leo took the bag upstairs to the smaller of his

two guestrooms just as his phone rang. It was Barrett again, and Leo nearly groaned. He'd spoken to his brother only about ten minutes ago, so something must have come up.

"This time I have good news," Barrett said the moment Leo answered.

"I'm definitely ready to hear some." Since Olivia was, too, Leo put the call on speaker.

"The psychiatrist is going to certify Milton competent to stand trial," his brother explained.

Leo certainly hadn't been expecting that. Everything they'd learned about Milton had pegged him as having mental issues. Apparently though, Milton did understand the judicial process and the charges that'd be levered against him.

"You're charging him with attempted murder of a police officer?" Leo asked.

"I am. I just told him this, and after he got past the shock, Milton said he wants to talk. He wants to tell us all about the person who's trying to kill you."

OLIVIA DIDN'T BOTHER to groan or huff. Yes, it was good news that Milton finally realized he was in scalding hot water and would likely spend the rest of his miserable life in jail.

But she felt another ploy coming on.

Another attempt to get Leo and her out into the open, maybe so one of Milton's cohorts could try to murder them.

Apparently, Leo felt the same way because he

huffed and muttered something profane. "I'm not taking Olivia back to the sheriff's office," he insisted. "It's getting dark, and I don't want her outside."

"I agree," Barrett said as fast as Leo had objected. "No need for it. When Milton insisted on talking to the two of you, I told him he'd have to do that with a video call. I can have that set up in just a couple of minutes if you want to hear what he has to say."

"Oh, we want to hear," Leo assured him. "And who knows, this time Milton might stop playing games long enough to give us some real info. Has he asked for a plea deal?" he added.

"Of course. That was one of the first things out of his mouth. I told him that I'd consider a deal if he actually gave us anything we could use to convict the person who hired him."

Good. Because Olivia didn't want Milton to walk unless they had his boss in custody. It twisted at her to think that the boss might be her father. Still, if he'd done these horrible things, then she wouldn't want him anywhere but behind bars.

"I'll call you after I have everything set up," Barrett said right before he clicked off.

Leo put aside his phone so he could set up one of the laptops that he apparently intended to use for the video call. While he was doing that, Olivia took a moment to go check on Cameron. He was splashing in the tub in the nursery bathroom, and she gave him a quick kiss.

"Is everything okay?" Izzie asked her.

Olivia nodded. "There might be a break in the case."

And Olivia hoped that wasn't all wishful thinking. Still, she held on to the hope that they'd soon have the name of the person responsible for terrorizing them. Then they could all deal with the fallout. Even if it wasn't her father who'd done this, it was someone she knew. Someone he'd trusted.

When Olivia made it back to the guest room, Leo already had the laptop booted up and she could see the camera feed of the interview room on the screen. The room was empty, but that changed almost immediately as Barrett ushered in Milton. Barrett had kept the man cuffed. A good thing, as far as Olivia was concerned. She didn't want Milton using this as a chance to try to escape.

"This is being recorded," Barrett told Milton. "And I've already read you your rights. I need you to say on record that you understand those rights and that you're waiving your right to an attorney."

"Yeah, I understand all that stuff. Are Leo and Olivia listening?" Milton immediately asked.

"We are," Leo said. "You'd better not be wasting our time."

"I'm not. I swear I'm not." Milton looked straight into the camera. "But I need a deal. I need immunity."

"You're not getting a free ride," Barrett assured him. "I've already told you the only deal you're getting is that I'll put in a good word for you with the DA if you give us your boss. That's it, Milton. That's the best you'll get from me."

Milton shook his head, muttered something Olivia didn't catch. *Great.* He was going to clam up again, or so Olivia thought. But the man's gaze zoomed to Barrett.

"You've got to swear to me that you'll work your butt off to get me a lighter sentence. Swear it," Milton repeated.

Barrett gave him a flat look. "You tried to kill my brother, and because you withheld information, it resulted in another attack, one where Olivia and my nephew could have been hurt. Added to that, there are two people dead. Working my butt off for you isn't high on my priority list. But," Barrett quickly added, "help me arrest the person behind the attacks, and I'll spell out to the DA that you're just a lackey."

Olivia thought that maybe Milton would be insulted with the term "lackey," but it seemed to make him relax a bit. Maybe because he thought being a hired gun would give him a lighter sentence than the person who'd hired him. She didn't think it would, though, and was pretty sure that accessory to murder, even after the fact, would carry the same penalty as murder itself.

"Okay," Milton said, gathering his breath. "I don't actually know the name of the person who hired me, but I can give you a description. He's in his thirties, is tall and has dark brown hair."

Well, that ruled out Bernice, Rena and her father,

but it must have triggered something for Barrett because he paused the interview. He then searched through something on his phone. When he obviously found what he was looking for, he turned the screen in Milton's direction.

"That's him," Milton said right off. "That's the guy who hired me."

Barrett shifted the phone screen so that Olivia and Leo could see, as well. It was Lowell, the dead gunman.

"What?" Milton asked when he noted the frustrated expression on Barrett's face. "That's the guy, I swear."

"He's dead," Barrett provided. "Now, I'm wondering if that's a nice coincidence for you so you can make us think that all of this is tied up in a neat little bow."

"No." Milton seemed adamant and repeated his denial when he looked at the laptop screen where he knew Leo and she were watching him. "He's dead? Who killed him?"

Olivia didn't think it was her imagination that the news had alarmed Milton. Maybe because he'd known Lowell. Or perhaps because he thought he might next in line to die.

"I had to shoot him," Leo answered. "To stop him from murdering Olivia and me. So, tell me why Lowell had it in for us and would hire you to come at me with a knife?"

"The only thing he said was that I could make

a lot of money if I took you out. I swear," Milton repeated, probably because Barrett was looking plenty skeptical.

Olivia was skeptical, as well. Milton would probably tell them anything to save his hide, and he'd withhold info, too, for that very same reason.

"Money?" Leo questioned. "That's why you agreed to kill me?"

Milton groaned and generally looked about as uncomfortable as a man could look. "I'm in trouble. I owe money to the wrong people, and I had to come up with some quick cash."

Leo jumped right on that. "How did you know Lowell? How'd he know you'd be willing to become a killer for hire?"

Milton shrugged. "I figured he worked for the men I owed the money. He just came up to me and asked if I wanted to get out of the hot water I was in. Not many people knew about my debts, so I just assumed he worked for the guys who'd lent me the funds."

"But you didn't find out for yourself?" Leo demanded.

"No. I was desperate. Those guys were going to kill me if I didn't pony up, so I saw the job Lowell offered as sort of self-defense."

That made Olivia sick to her stomach with disgust. This snake had been willing to end a good man's life to save his own one. And all because of money.

"How much did Lowell pay you?" she snapped. She wanted to add more, to blister him with some backlash from her temper, but that wouldn't help. It might even hurt if it caused Milton to realize how much trouble he was in and clam up.

Milton hesitated, and she could see the battle he was having with himself as to how much to tell them. He maybe thought he should paint himself in the best light possible, but he was well beyond that. There was no "light" that would make him appear to be a decent human being.

"Ten grand," Milton finally said.

Oh, that didn't help with her bubbling temper and disgust. For ten thousand dollars, Milton had been willing to kill Leo, and for her father, that would have been chump change. Maybe for Bernice, too. Olivia didn't know her financial situation but suspected that the woman had saved most of her high salary. Bernice had certainly never taken a vacation, and to the best of Olivia's knowledge, she didn't have any expensive jewelry. Didn't even have her own car. Whenever Bernice needed to leave the estate, she used one of the vehicles.

Like the one that'd been spotted around the same time as Randall's body dump.

Bernice could have been in that vehicle. Then again, her father used the same type of SUV. And if Rena had access to the estate, she could have been behind the wheel of one, too. The keys for the vehicles were kept in the ignitions while they were in the garage.

"And FYI," Milton added a moment later, "I didn't get the full payment. Lowell only gave me three thousand up front and said I'd get the rest when I finished the job. Then he made me do a confession of sorts so that I wouldn't renege on the deal and run with the cash that I had."

"A confession?" Barrett asked, jumping right on that.

Again, Milton hesitated before he explained. "Lowell used a phone to record it. He had me say my name and that I was going to kill Deputy Leo Logan."

Olivia exchanged a glance with Leo. He was probably wondering the same thing she was—whether Lowell had planned to set up Milton to take the fall for Leo and any other attacks. Milton certainly made a perfect fall guy, and as he'd admitted himself, he was desperate.

"From everything we've gathered so far, Lowell was a hired thug, too," Barrett pointed out. "So, who hired him?"

That put some fresh alarm on Milton's face. "I don't know. That's the truth," he added in protest over their groans.

Leo huffed. "If you don't know that, then you're wasting our time," he snapped. "No information, no good word for you with the DA." His tone made it sound as if he was about to end the video session.

"Wait!" Milton pleaded. "I've got something.

Something that should be worth more than just a good word with the DA."

"What?" Leo and Barrett asked at the same time, and both had plenty of skepticism in their expression. Olivia was right there with them.

"Lowell gave me a burner cell that he used to call me," Milton went on. "He told me to toss it right before I went after Leo, and I did."

"And how the heck is a burner going to help us?" Barrett fired back. "Lowell's dead, and what does it matter if he called you on it? He was probably using a burner himself."

"Probably," Milton admitted and then flashed an oily smile. "Lowell wasn't the only one who called me on it, though. I got another call, right before I went after Leo."

Suddenly, Olivia was very interested in what the man was saying. Leo, too, and they automatically moved closer to the laptop screen.

"Who called you?" Barrett urged.

The smile stayed on Milton's mouth. "The person didn't say who he or she was. The voice was all muffled-like. But the caller said Lowell was having trouble with his phone reception, but that I should go ahead and finish off Leo Logan."

There were indeed plenty of areas with bad reception near her place where the second attacker—Lowell—had likely gone. Someone had fired shots into her house shortly after Leo had arrived.

"I'm betting that caller was Lowell's boss," Milton insisted.

Barrett stared at him. "Let me guess. You have no idea where you tossed this burner phone."

"Oh, I know, all right. And this really oughta be worth more than just a word with the DA."

Obviously, Milton wanted to use this as a further bargaining tool, but Barrett just shook his head. "So far, you've given us little to nothing. Give me something now, or you're going back to your cell."

"All right," Milton said after what was obviously a mental debate with himself. "I figured if I could finish off Leo all quiet-like, then I could go back and get the burner and my own phone, which Lowell said I wasn't to have on me during the attack. So, I hid my cell and the burner in the bushes in the back of the parking lot and covered them with some leaves."

With his restraints rattling, he motioned toward the side of the building where there was indeed a parking lot. One with a row of hedges at the back.

"Go ahead and look," Milton insisted. "You'll see the number of the person who called me on the burner. Then you can listen to the conversation on my phone."

"You recorded it?" Leo asked before Olivia could jump right on that.

Milton's smile widened. "I did with my own phone. Listen to it, and you'll hear the voice of the person who wants you dead."

## Chapter Fourteen

Leo wished he could be in two places at once. He wanted to be at the sheriff's office, helping Barrett look for those two phones Milton had claimed he'd tossed. But Leo couldn't do that at the possible expense of Cameron and Olivia. Just because Lowell was dead and Milton was in restraints, it didn't mean the person who'd hired them hadn't sent another killer after them.

Olivia was pacing across the guest room, so obviously she was on edge, too, while they waited for word from Barrett. They had used some of their waiting time to go into the nursery to say goodnight to Cameron. Leo had also brought in some covers for Izzie who'd insisted on using the sleep chair next to Cameron's crib. That was good because Cameron wouldn't be alone, but Leo figured when he and Olivia finally went to bed, they'd be bunking in the nursery, as well.

Leo checked the time and cursed when he realized it was only two minutes later than when he'd last checked. It hadn't been long—less that fifteen minutes—since Milton had told them about the phones, so it wasn't as if Barrett was dragging his feet on this. Plus, it was possible that the phones weren't where Milton had said they were.

Or they might not even exist.

The sigh he heard from Olivia told Leo that she was probably stressing over the same thing.

"Milton would be stupid to lie about this," Leo told her, though it probably wasn't much assurance because Milton clearly wasn't a smart man. Still, Leo could see how a stall tactic would help him.

"He or she," Olivia muttered. She stopped pacing and turned toward him. "That's what Jace said about the person who'd called him with the anonymous tip about Randall's body."

Leo nodded. Yeah, he'd remembered that, and if an indistinguishable muffled voice was all they had, then this wouldn't be much of a lead. Then again, he or Olivia might recognize something. Maybe even some background noise.

"Even if these phones end up ID'ing the killer," Olivia said, "I want Milton in jail. I want him to pay for what he did to you."

Yeah, but more than that, Leo wanted the person who was pulling the strings. Or rather, pulling the trigger. Because that's what this person was—a killer.

Because she looked as if her nerves were worse than his, Leo went to her and pulled her into his arms. He'd stopped trying to talk himself out of doing stuff like this. Plain and simple, he didn't even want to try to keep resisting Olivia.

He could hear the whirl of the AC, feel the cool air spilling on them. Feel the heat of her body, too. And her warm breath hitting against his neck.

Leo gave her another of those cheek kisses, but she didn't exactly melt against him. She was definitely wired, not only by the wait but from the stress of the constant threat of danger. The tension went up a significant notch when his phone rang.

Even though Leo had been anticipating the call, he still bobbled his phone when he yanked it from his jeans. Barrett's name was on the screen, so Leo answered it as fast as he could.

"I found the cells," Barrett said, his voice pouring through the room as Leo put the call on speaker. "They were right where Milton told us they'd be."

Leo released a long breath. "That's a good start. Please tell me he actually recorded his boss giving the order to kill me."

"He did. I've only listened to it once, so all I can tell you is that the voice is indeed muffled. Barely audible, in fact. But I'll send it to you so you can hear it for yourself."

Leo was certain both Barrett and he would be listening to it multiple times. So would the crime lab.

"I expected the caller to be using a burner, too," Barrett continued a moment later. "He or she didn't."

Olivia made a small gasping sound. "You know who made the call?" she blurted.

"No, but I know where the call originated," Barrett corrected. "It came from a landline at your father's estate."

It took Leo a moment to wrap his mind around that, and he didn't like the conclusions he reached. "Lowell gave Milton a burner, but the person who hired them didn't take that simple step to cover his tracks?"

"Yes," Barrett agreed.

It was obvious they thought that maybe this was some kind of stupid scheme meant to make Samuel look guilty.

"It's just like the vehicle," Olivia said. Her forehead was furrowed, the worry plentiful in her eyes. "Any of the three could have used a landline phone in the house."

Bingo. That could have been intentional or an oversight. After all, maybe the culprit hadn't thought Milton would record the call or ditch the phone so it could so easily be found.

"I'll get a warrant to access the phone lines at the estate," Barrett advised. "After I have the info I need on the calls, I'll question Samuel, Rena and Bernice again in the morning. In the meantime, listen to the call and let me know if you hear anything that I've missed."

A moment later, Leo's phone dinged with the recording Barrett had just sent him. Leo ended the call with his brother so that he and Olivia could listen to it.

"Lowell's got bad phone reception," the caller said. Either Milton hadn't managed to record the "greeting" or there hadn't been one. "Do the job on Leo Logan, and when we have proof it's done, you'll get the rest of your money."

That was it. No flashing neon light of information, and Barrett and Milton had been right about the voice. It was muffled and, to Leo's ear, indistinguishable. Apparently, it was the same for Olivia because she cursed, as well.

Leo hit Replay, listened, and then hit Replay again. On the fourth listen, Olivia sank onto the foot of the bed and shook her head.

"I hear some background noise," she said, "but it only sounds like wind blowing or maybe a ceiling fan."

"Same here," Leo agreed. And if it was indeed wind, it could have been coming from the parking lot of the sheriff's office. In other words, no help whatsoever.

He sank beside her, took her hand and tried to put at least some positive spin on things. "Once Barrett gets the warrant and the phone records from the estate, we might be able to pinpoint which landline was used."

Though he figured there were many extensions off a single line, he thought it best not to remind Olivia of that since she already looked as if she was about to crash and burn. He knew how she felt. He'd clung to the hope that the phones would give them a solid clue. And *that* they had. The call had come from the estate, which meant the killer had been there. That wasn't a surprise, but maybe they could use the phone records and compare them to the alibis or statements of their suspects.

Or they could bluff.

"Barrett's allowed to lie in interview," Leo explained. "He could bring in Rena, Bernice and Samuel, tell them that Milton recorded the order for the hit on me, and the person responsible might break."

*"Might,"* she repeated in a mumble.

Even though it hadn't helped with the stress the other times he'd done it, Leo pulled her into his arms again.

"I wish Barrett could arrest them all," she added.

Yeah, too bad he couldn't do it. But even that might not end the danger because there could already be other hired guns out there, waiting for their shot. When Olivia pulled back and met his gaze, he knew that she was well aware of that scenario, too.

"We should listen to the recording again," she said, not breaking eye contact with him. "We also need to go over my mother's journals. And brainstorm as to why Bernice, Rena or my father wants us dead."

They did indeed need to do all those things. But Leo went for something totally different.

He kissed her.

Again, there was no *melting*. In fact, Olivia went stiff, and he figured she would put a quick stop to this. After all, kissing wasn't one of the options she'd just spelled out for what they should be doing.

The weariness was still in her eyes. Actually, on every part of her face, and because he had his arms around her, Leo could feel the knotted muscles in her back.

"Bad timing," he said and started to move away from her.

Olivia stopped him by catching the front of his T-shirt. "The timing is awful," she agreed. "Plenty of things are awful. You're not. This isn't."

And this time, she kissed him.

Leo didn't stop her. He wasn't an idiot. This was exactly what he wanted. He could even try to make himself believe that it'd be a great stress reliever. A way for them to forget the hell they'd been going through. Well, forget it for a short time anyway. But this wasn't about stress or forgetting. This kiss was about giving in to the heat that they'd both been fighting for way too long.

She was the one who deepened the kiss, threading her fingers into his hair, bringing him closer to her. Not that Leo needed any such adjustments to get him closer. He had already headed in that direction and made some adjustments of his own so that her breasts landed against his chest.

The kiss continued, but he added some touching to this make-out session. He slipped his hand between them, cupped her breasts and swiped his thumb over her nipple. The silky sound of pleasure Olivia made nearly brought him to his knees. Thankfully, though, it didn't rid him of common sense. He stood, leading her with him to the door so he could lock it. No way did he want Izzie walking in on them.

Even with all the moving around, Olivia didn't miss a beat, and she didn't haul him back to the bed. Instead, she pushed him so that his back landed against the wall and she went in for a kiss that was well past the make-out stage. This was a carnal invitation to sex.

And Leo's body responded.

He went hard as stone, and every part of him urged him to strip off her clothes and take her now, now, now. Leo wanted *now* more than he wanted air in his lungs, but he didn't want to take Olivia in some frantic coupling. It would leave them both sated, that was for sure. However, it would be over way too fast. He didn't want fast. He wanted—no, he *needed*—to hang on to this even if just for the night.

"Your arm," she said out of the blue. "You're hurt."

"I'm not hurting," he told her. That was the truth. He wasn't sure he could feel a mountain of pain right now.

"You're sure?" she pressed.

He took her hand and put it over his erection. "I'm sure."

She smiled. A sly, wicked smile, and kept her hand in place. "I haven't had you in over a year and a half."

She looked at him. Her eyes hot now. The need had replaced the weariness and fatigue. He thought for a second that she was going to tell him they needed to rethink this, that there were reasons why they'd been apart for over a year and a half. That there were reasons, like the investigation, why they should table this and go back to it when Barrett had made an arrest.

"A year and a half is too long," she said.

Her voice was a throaty whisper. Like the rest of her, it tugged and pulled at him until Leo felt the snap. The one that told him he wouldn't be able to draw this out, after all. The *now* was going to win.

So, he took her now. He kissed her, the hunger and need clawing through him. Through her, too. Because she kicked off her shoes and began to tug at his shirt. Leo helped her with that and did the same to hers. Their tops landed on the floor. He unhooked the front clasp of her bra and tossed it down with the other items of clothing. This wouldn't be pretty, but they'd get it done.

Suddenly her hands were on him. On his bare chest. His back. Touching him. Making him crazy. The craziness climbed when she went after the zipper of his jeans. *Now* was winning for her, too, but through all of that, she made sure she didn't touch his wounded arm.

He backed her toward the bed. Kissing her. With skin sliding against skin. Her nipples were too much to resist, so he dipped his head and took one into his mouth. His reward was that she made that silky moan of pleasure again and bucked against him.

They fell onto the bed together.

Leo kept tugging at her nipple and then he kissed his way down her stomach. To her jeans, which he shimmied off her. Her panties came next, and he did even more kissing. Pleasing her. Pleasing himself.

"Don't mention the stretch marks," she muttered.

Because his pulse was throbbing in his ears, it took him a moment to realize what she'd said. Since his mouth was still right there, he kissed the marks, as well.

"If you think they're a turn-off, you're wrong," he told her. Just the opposite. She'd had his child, their son, and the marks were a reminder of that.

Olivia made a sound that let him know that she wasn't quite convinced. Leo would have *convinced* her, too, but she rolled on top of him. Again, she was mindful of his arm.

"I don't want you reopening the cut," she said, levering to straddle him and go after his zipper.

Leo was about to insist that he wasn't concerned about the damn cut, but then she got off his jeans. Got off his boxers. And nearly got him off when her hands skimmed over him.

He gritted his teeth and let her do what she wanted. Apparently some kisses and touching as he'd done. Or maybe she was just trying to drive him insane. She nearly managed it, too, before she finally made her way back up his body and, sliding her hips against his, took him inside her.

Now he had to grit his teeth from the sheer pleasure of the sensations firing through him. Mercy, the woman was good at this.

Olivia stilled, giving them both a moment to catch their breath. She waited until their eyes were locked before she braced her hands on his chest and started to move. She was good at this, too, but there was no way Leo could just lie there and not get involved. He caught her hips, adding some pressure to those thrusts that would soon push them both right over the edge.

His body begged for release while he also tried to hold on. To make this last as long as possible. He was doing a decent job of it when he felt the orgasm ripple through Olivia. She fisted around him, giving him no choice but to give in to the need.

Leo pulled her down to him and followed her.

## Chapter Fifteen

Olivia lay on top of Leo and tried to level her breathing. Tried to shut out the thoughts, too. She succeeded in doing the first but failed big-time with the second. The thoughts came. Both good and bad.

Making love with Leo had been something starved for. It'd been like coming home, Christmas and her birthday all rolled into one.

And that was the problem.

Great sex only made her want him more, and while he certainly seemed able to put their past troubles behind him, they had a very rough road ahead of them. One that might involve her own father's arrest for attempting to murder them. Even if it wasn't Samuel, she and Leo wouldn't have an easy time putting aside everything that'd happen and just move on with their lives.

Besides, Leo might not want to "move on" with her.

He'd certainly not said anything about an ever-after or even a commitment. Of course, they had a commitment because of Cameron, but being with

Leo like this made Olivia realize that she wanted more. She wanted the whole package. Leo. Their son. A life together.

Even though the timing was lousy for it, Olivia worked up enough steel to open that "life together" conversation with him. Best not to do that, however, while he was still inside her, so she eased off him, mindful not to touch his arm, and dropped onto the bed so they were side to side. She pulled the edge of the quilt over her and looked at him.

Just as he cursed.

It wasn't a mild oath, either, and she figured it had to be aimed at her. Or rather, their situation. Mercy. Here she was fantasizing about a life with him, and he probably thought this had been a huge mistake.

"No condom," he groaned.

Olivia blinked. Then her eyes went wide when his words sank in. She practically snapped to a sitting position and stared down at him.

"Yeah," Leo said, obviously noting the extreme shock that had to be on her face. He straightened, as well, groaned and cursed some more. "I'm so sorry."

She opened her mouth but wasn't sure what to say. This wasn't something she could just blow off and tell him not to worry about. Still, she could give him a little reassurance about one possible pitfall to not practicing safe sex.

"I'm okay," she said. "I mean I've been tested, and I haven't been with anyone since you."

He turned his head, slowly, his gaze snaring hers. "No one in nearly two years?"

Olivia realized that it sounded as if she was stuck on him and unable to move on to anyone else.

And that was the truth.

However, since it was the truth, she didn't intend to admit it to him, not now when declaring her feelings for him would be the last thing he'd want to hear.

"No one," she verified. "I stay really busy with Cameron. I don't have time for a relationship."

He just continued to stare at her with those stone-gray eyes. Eyes that seemed to see right through her to suss out the lie she'd just told. Yes, she was busy, but she hadn't wanted another man. Hadn't wanted to be with anyone other than Leo and maybe would have been had it not been for her father.

"I haven't been with anyone since you, either," he said.

Olivia was certain her look of shock returned, intensified. She nearly laughed because it seemed a joke that someone who was at hot as Leo would go that long without having a woman. But he was serious.

Cursing again, he rubbed his hand over his face and then groaned. "No condom," he repeated as if to get them back on track with the conversation. Apparently, he didn't want to launch into a discussion of why they'd been living celibate lives. "Any chance you can tell me it's the wrong time of the month?"

No chance whatsoever, and that's why Olivia settled for a shrug. Her cycle hadn't been regular since she'd had Cameron so, as far as she knew, there was no such thing as the wrong time of the month.

"It'll be okay," she insisted though she had absolutely nothing to back it up. Well, nothing except what would certainly sound like lame logic. "We used protection before, and I still got pregnant with Cameron, so maybe that means the odds are in our favor that I won't get pregnant now."

He turned to stare at her again. A flat stare that told her he'd had no trouble figuring out the "lame" part. But the turning and staring put his face very close to hers and, despite this serious concern, Olivia felt a little weak in the knees just looking at him. Here, only minutes had passed since she'd had him and she wanted him all over again.

Olivia leaned in and saw the surprise flash in his eyes before she kissed him. She'd thought he'd resist. After all, they had work to do, and there was that whole part about them literally having had sex just minutes earlier. But he didn't resist. Leo muttered something she didn't catch, slid his hand around the back of her neck and hauled her to him. She laughed, kept kissing him and slid back onto his lap.

The kiss turned instantly hot. Then again, it wasn't possible to kiss Leo and not feel the heat. But this time they didn't get to push it any further. That's because Leo stopped.

"I think I hear something," Leo said, causing her laughter, and the heat, to vanish. "I need to talk to the ranch hand."

He swore when he reached for his phone and it wasn't there. That's because it was in jeans' pocket and all their clothes were scattered on the floor. As soon as they got off the bed and located it in his jeans by the nightstand, Leo made the call.

"Wally," Leo greeted. "Is something wrong?"

Alarmed at Leo's tone, Olivia moved closer to hear, but Leo fixed that by putting the call on speaker so that it'd free up his hands to pull on his jeans.

"Maybe," Wally answered. "There's someone walking up the road toward the house. Or rather, staggering. I can't tell who it is, but it is a woman."

Olivia certainly hadn't been expecting Wally to say that. Her worst fear was that he had been about to tell them he'd spotted a gunman. That's why Olivia had practically been throwing on her clothes so she could hurry to Cameron. But this didn't seem like an immediate threat.

Well, maybe it wasn't.

It quickly occurred to her that it could be some kind of ruse. Something set up so an attacker could get closer to the house.

"Is the woman armed?" Leo asked the hand.

"I don't think so. She's not carrying a purse or anything…hell, she just fell down. Should I go out and check on her?"

Olivia saw the sleek muscle tighten in Leo's jaw and knew he was debating how to handle this. His ranch was miles from town, so he didn't normally get foot traffic out here. However, it could be someone who'd been in a car accident and was looking for help.

"Wait," Wally said a moment later. "She's getting up and looking up at the house. She's coming this way, boss."

"Don't go check on her yourself," Leo instructed. "Send two of the other hands and make sure to tell them to be careful. We have two women who are suspects, so whoever it is, she could be armed and dangerous. Report back to me as soon as you know who she is."

"Will do," Wally assured him.

The moment Leo ended the call, he finished getting dressed and motioned for Olivia to follow him. "Tell Izzie to take Cameron and get in the tub with him. I'm going to the front windows to see if I can spot our visitor."

Olivia hated to alarm Cameron or Izzie, but when she hurried into the nursery, she could see that Cameron was asleep. She relayed Leo's orders and then tried to reassure Izzie that it was simply a precaution.

She prayed that's exactly what it was—a precaution.

Once she'd helped Izzie move Cameron into the bathroom, Olivia rushed back out to find Leo. He was in his office, a room on the second floor at the front of the house. He had a pair of binoculars pressed to his eyes and was looking out the window. She hurried to him, but he motioned for her to stay to the side. That, of course, was so that she wouldn't be in the line of fire. Unlike Leo. He was standing there, his weapon drawn and ready for whatever was about to happen.

"I can't tell if it's Bernice or Rena," he told her. "But two hands are in a truck and heading her way."

Olivia stayed to the side of the window, but peered around the frame, hoping to get a glimpse of what was happening. She did. She saw the headlights of the truck making its way down the road. Several moments later, the truck stopped, and the headlights shone right on the woman.

"It's Bernice," Leo muttered. "She's got blood on her face."

So, maybe the car accident theory was right. Except that wouldn't explain what Bernice was doing out here in the first place.

Olivia continued to watch as both men got out of the truck and walked toward the woman. Bernice fell forward, practically collapsing, before one of them caught her. The second man took out his phone and, seconds later, Leo's phone rang. He put the call on speaker and it didn't take long for the ranch hand's voice to pour through the room.

"The woman says her name is Bernice Saylor," the hand explained. "And she says she needs to see you. She claims that that somebody ran her off the road and then tried to kill her."

LEO HAD ALREADY cursed way too much tonight, so he didn't add more. Though this was definitely a situation that called for profanity.

And caution.

His first instinct was to dismiss this as some kind of dangerous ploy for Bernice to get to him, but then Leo thought of Randall. He, too, had said someone had tried to kill him.

That someone had succeeded, too.

Leo didn't want to take the risk that the same thing would happen with Bernice. Especially if the woman was innocent. But he would need to add some layers of security to the help he gave her.

"I'm calling Barrett," Leo told the hand, Carter Johnson. "Stay put until I do that."

He hadn't even had time to end the call with Carter when there was a loud blast and a fireball shot up from the pasture just to the right of where his ranch hands were standing with Bernice. The two men dropped to the ground, pulling Bernice down with them.

"What the hell?" he heard Carter grumble just as Bernice shouted, "She's trying to kill me."

At least that's what Leo thought they'd said before their voices were drowned out by another blast. Then another. All three flare-ups had been in the pastures, too far from the house to do any damage, but his two hands and Bernice could be in immediate danger.

"Check to make sure Bernice isn't armed," Leo instructed Carter when he came back on the line. "If she's not, put her in the truck and drive her to the house, but don't bring her in. Get out of there fast," he added when there was a fourth blast.

"The flames aren't big enough to burn through the pasture grass," Leo tried to assure Olivia. "But I'll call the fire department anyway."

"I'll do that," Olivia volunteered, taking his phone. "You keep watch."

He didn't turn down her offer because keeping watch was critical right now. Leo doubted that the person who'd set those fires had actually been close enough to light them. No, the fireballs were probably on some kind of timer or device, the way the one in Randall's truck had been. There hadn't been time for Leo to send the hands into the pastures to look for any devices, but clearly there'd been some.

"Tell the fire department to approach with caution, that there could be a sniper in the area," Leo rattled off to her. "And then call Barrett to let him know what's going on. Same rules apply to him," he insisted. "I don't want him caught in the crosshairs of a gunman."

Olivia gave him a nod, a very shaky one, and her hands were trembling a little, but she made the calls. Leo half listened to her relay what he'd told her to say, but he kept his focus on his ranch hands and Bernice. She didn't protest when Carter frisked her. He must not have found any weapons because, seconds after, he all but carried Bernice to the truck and put her inside.

Another fireball shot up. This one was at the end of the drive, and it was different from the others.

Those first ones had been blasts, but this was more of a line of fire that created a wall to prevent someone from getting to or from the house. It was as if someone had poured gasoline onto the asphalt and then lit it. Of course, that could have been done with a timer, as well.

And that was also why he had no intention of trusting Bernice.

Olivia was still on the phone with Barrett when the truck started toward the house. The lights slashed through the darkness, and Leo used that light to try to glimpse anyone who might have managed to sneak onto the grounds. He didn't see anyone, but that didn't mean someone wasn't out there. That's why he wanted Izzie to stay put with Cameron until he was certain the place was secure.

"Oh God," he heard Olivia say.

Leo whipped toward her. "What's wrong?" he demanded.

"Barrett was leaving his house and a firebomb went off at the end of his driveway."

Hell. Leo knew that wasn't a coincidence. "Is Della there with him?"

"Yes," Olivia verified, her voice now shaking as much as the rest of her.

"Then tell Barrett to stay put," Leo insisted.

Barrett's fiancée, Della, was pregnant, and Leo didn't want to put her or their baby at risk by Barrett leaving her alone. Della was a deputy sheriff and could likely take care of herself, but the person behind these attacks could try to take Della hostage and use her as leverage. Leo couldn't do that to Della or Barrett.

"See if Daniel can come," Leo told her. "But let him know what he could be up against and tell him that he'll have to use the trails to get here."

Olivia finished her call with Barrett and made the one to Daniel just as Leo watched Carter pull the truck to a stop in front of the house. Not too close, though. And there was a lot of open yard between the vehicle and the house. If Bernice got out and tried to run toward them, there'd be plenty of ranch hands to stop her.

He heard the soft ding on his phone to indicate an incoming call. A moment later Olivia said, "It's Carter." Handing him his phone, she added, "Daniel's coming ASAP."

Leo had no doubts that Daniel would indeed try to get here fast, but he had to wonder if there'd be another fire. Another distraction. Something that would stop backup from getting to the ranch.

"Carter," Leo said when he took the incoming call. "What's going on?"

"The woman wasn't armed," the ranch hand answered. "That's about all I know right now. That, and what she's saying about somebody trying to kill her. But I don't know who set those fires. I didn't see anybody, boss, and I've been keeping watch for hours."

"The fires could have been rigged days ago," Leo

explained. In fact, they could have been set even before the one that'd taken out Randall's truck. The bomb squad hadn't gone out into the pastures to look for more devices because they'd concentrated on the house and the outbuildings.

"Put Bernice on the phone," Leo instructed Carter.

It didn't take long for Carter to do that and Leo soon heard Bernice. "Thank you for saving me," the woman blustered, her words running together. "She nearly killed me."

Leo had plenty of questions, but he started with the big one. "Who tried to kill you?"

"Rena." Bernice didn't hesitate, either. "She ran me off the road and then tried to shoot me. I got away from her."

"Rena," he repeated, both skeptical and curious. He didn't doubt that Rena was capable of doing something like this, but he also had no doubt that Bernice could be lying. "Where did all of this happen?"

"Just up the main road, not far from your ranch. I was coming here because of Samuel. He's distraught, and I thought I could talk Olivia into calling him. I guess Rena followed me."

Leo didn't press the point that it was a stupid idea for Bernice to try to convince Olivia to call her father. There were too many other things he needed to know. Obviously, things that Olivia should know, as well, because she was leaning closer to listen to the conversation. Leo didn't want her in front of the window so he switched the call to speaker.

"You're sure it was Rena who ran you off the road?" Leo pressed. "You saw her?"

Now, Bernice paused. "Not exactly. But I saw the logo on the door of the SUV. Rena was at the estate, and she must have taken it."

Maybe. Or it could have been Samuel in the vehicle. The man might have had motive to off his estate manager after what'd gone on between them in the sheriff's office. Then again, maybe Bernice and Samuel had mended fences if she was telling the truth about trying to convince Olivia to speak to him.

But that was a big *if*.

"Stay put in the truck with my ranch hands," Leo told Bernice. "And I mean stay put. I'm going to call Rena to see if I can get her side of this."

"She'll just lie," Bernice insisted. "She'll say I made it all up."

Yeah, she might, but Leo ended the call with Bernice. Since he didn't have Rena's number handy, he worked his way through the dispatcher to have the deputy place the call. During that wait, he also looked at Olivia to make sure she was okay.

She wasn't.

All of this was giving her another slam of fear, and he hated to see it in her eyes. Hated that he wouldn't be able to stop it until he'd worked out this situation with Bernice and now Rena.

"You could wait in the nursery," he suggested. "You could be with Cameron."

She glanced at the doorway. Then back at him. And Olivia shook her head. "No one can get into the nursery without us knowing. The security alarm would go off if someone tried to get into the house."

He nodded and would have tried to give her some kind of assurance that everything would be okay, but the call to Rena finally went through. The phone rang and rang, and just when Leo figured a voice mail recording would kick in, she answered. Or rather, someone did.

"I'm hurt."

It was a woman, and it was possible it was Rena. It was hard to tell, however, because the voice was muffled—a reminder of the other calls that had been mentioned in this investigation.

"Rena?" he asked.

"Yes, it's me. I'm hurt," she repeated.

A muffled voice as well as injuries could be faked, and Leo had no idea if that was the case. "Where are you? What happened?"

"I'm hurt," she repeated. "Help me."

Leo frowned because she hadn't answered either of his questions. He tried again. "I'll help you as soon as you tell me where you are."

Of course, he could try to have the call traced and her location pinpointed by using the cell towers, but all of that would take time.

There was a long silence before Rena muttered,

"I'm in one of your pastures, I think. I think I can see the lights from your house."

Hell. He didn't want her that close, and it really didn't help him pinpoint her location since he had hundreds of acres of pastures. Plus, it was possible that the lights she was seeing weren't from his house but rather one of the outbuildings.

"How'd you get in my pasture?" he snapped.

"Um, I was looking for Samuel." Her breath was pitched and labored.

Well, that seemed to be tonight's trend for the women in Samuel's life. Leo didn't bother to ask her why she thought Samuel would be at his place.

"Use the landline," he instructed Olivia, tipping his head to the phone on his desk. "Call an ambulance and tell the EMTs what Rena just said. But they need to approach with caution."

"Because this could be a trap," Olivia supplied with a nod.

"Not a trap." Rena's voice was even more slurred now than when she'd first answered. In fact, if this was an act, she was doing a damn good job of it.

"The ambulance is on the way," Olivia relayed several moments later.

"You hear that?" Leo asked Rena as he kept watch out the window. Because this entire conversation could be a distraction so that someone could sneak onto the ranch. "An ambulance will be here soon. What are your injuries?"

There were some moans, and it sounded as if she

was moving around. "My head. Everything's spinning around. And I'm bleeding. God, I'm bleeding."

"Tell me what happened," Leo persisted.

"I'm not sure. I was driving and everything started spinning. My head's bleeding. I'm hurt, so I must have wrecked. I wrecked and then I got out and started walking to get help."

"You could have used your phone to call 9-1-1," he pointed out.

"Not thinking straight. So dizzy." There was a thud. It sounded as if Rena had fallen.

Leo wasn't ready to give up. Besides, he needed to keep Rena on the phone until the EMTs arrived and managed to find her. If she was talking, they might be able to hear the sound of her voice. However, he did have to wonder if she'd been drugged— just as Simone had been. But that was something he'd need to figure out later.

"Did you just try to kill Bernice?" Leo demanded. "She said you did."

"Bernice?" she mumbled.

"That's right. Bernice. Did you try to kill her?" he asked.

"No." She muttered some things he couldn't make out. "But I know who tried to kill you."

"Who?" Leo snapped.

Nothing. No moans, no more sounds of Rena moving around.

"Rena?" Leo said. "Say something. Keep talking to me."

Still nothing, and that started a war within him. If Rena was indeed hurt, he needed to get to her to try to save her life. But he couldn't leave Olivia, Cameron and Izzie. He certainly couldn't leave them long enough to go wandering around his pastures, looking for Rena.

"I need to talk to Bernice," he declared. "Not on the phone. I need to get in her face to see for myself if she knows what's going on."

Olivia touched her fingers to her lips for a moment. Obviously, she was having the same internal battle as he was. Except she had the added concern of not wanting him to get hurt.

"I'll get Carter to move the truck closer to the house so I won't have to cross the yard," Leo explained. "And I'll have him wait inside with you until I'm done with Bernice. You can stay up here but keep away from the windows." He paused, hating to add this last part since he knew it was only going to put more alarm on her face. "There's a gun on the top shelf of the closet." He tipped his head to the door just a few feet away from his desk.

Olivia nodded, and because he figured they both could use it, he gave her a quick kiss. Leo pulled back, looked at her. And then gave her another kiss that wasn't so quick.

"I won't be long," he said and hoped that was true.

Keeping his gun ready, he called Carter while he went downstairs. Leo waited at the front door until the hand had moved the truck right up to the porch.

Even then Leo waited until Carter was out and at the door before he disarmed the security system to let the hand in.

"No matter what happens," Leo told him, "protect Olivia, Cameron and Izzie."

"I will, boss," Carter assured him.

Leo dragged in a long breath and, hoping this wasn't a huge mistake, stepped outside and hurried to the truck. He got in behind the wheel and immediately turned to face Bernice who was in the center with the other hand, Edwin Dade, on the passenger's side.

Bernice did have blood on her face, along with some cuts and scrapes. None looked serious. Being the skeptical cop that he was, Leo decided they could have been self-inflicted.

"Start talking," Leo told Bernice. "You said Rena tried to kill you, and I want details."

"Of course." Bernice took her own deep breath.

But before she could say a word, all hell broke loose and the front end of the truck exploded.

OLIVIA'S HEART WENT to her knees when she heard the blast. This one was much louder than the others, and when she glanced out the window of Leo's office, she saw smoke and flames shoot out from the truck.

Oh God.

Someone had used a firebomb on the truck, and Leo was inside it.

She hurried out of the office, made it halfway down the stairs before she saw the thick black smoke. Not only in the truck now. It was billowing in through the front door where Carter stood. "Go help Leo," she insisted.

Carter had already started in that direction, and Olivia went down the rest of the stairs to look out to see if she could spot Leo. She couldn't. She couldn't even tell how much of the truck was still intact. It could be blown to bits.

Leo could be dead.

The hoarse sob left her throat. Tears stung her eyes. But then so did the smoke and it wasn't long before she started to cough. She had no choice but to close the door because she couldn't breathe. She also couldn't risk the smoke and fire getting to Cameron.

As much as she wanted to see Leo, Olivia knew she had to protect their son. She raced back up the stairs, going straight to the nursery. The fist around her heart loosened a little when she saw that her baby was asleep in Izzie's arms.

"What happened?" Izzie asked.

Olivia couldn't speak. Her throat had clamped shut and her fear for Leo was skyrocketing.

"Just stay put," she managed to tell Izzie. She ran back out, racing into Leo's office so she could get a better look at the truck.

She cursed the smoke that had blanketed the entire front yard and the front of the house, but she could see someone moving around. Carter, she realized when, a moment later, he pulled someone from the truck.

Leo.

Mercy, Leo looked unconscious, or worse, and the hand had to drag him away from the burning truck. She reached for the landline to call an ambulance, only to remember that one was already on the way. So was the fire department. Maybe they would both get here soon. And while she was hoping, she added a plea that the EMTs would be able to get past that fire on the road. It was still blazing, as were the ones in the pasture. But those fires didn't have the thick smoke like the one in the truck.

Olivia continued to keep watch, knowing that she was breaking Leo's order for her to stay away from the windows. She couldn't. She had to see if he was all right; it crushed her to think that she could lose him.

She was in love with him and had been since they'd first become lovers. Olivia knew that now— for all the good it'd do because she might not get a chance to ever tell him.

There was more movement in the smoke, but she lost sight of where Carter had taken Leo. She lost sight of pretty much anything when the smoke billowed up, blocking any view she had from the window.

But Olivia could still hear.

And she heard something that put her body on full alert.

She hadn't seen anyone come into the house, but she was pretty sure she heard footsteps in the foyer. Then the front door closing. She nearly rushed back downstairs to see if it was Leo, but everything inside her warned her that it wasn't.

Someone was in the house.

Someone who could try to kill her and get to Cameron.

Everything froze for a moment. Her feet. Her breath. Maybe even her heart. But nothing stopped the fear that shot like icy fingers up her spine.

She forced herself to stay quiet. To think. And she remembered Leo telling her about the gun. Stepping as softly as she could, she went to his office closet and, moving to her tiptoes, felt around until she found it. She'd had some firearms training— *some*—and prayed that she remembered it. Maybe, just maybe, it wouldn't even be necessary.

With the gun gripped in her hands, Olivia made her way to the office door and looked out. The smoke was still there, thick in the foyer and drifting up the stairs. There were just enough breaks in the drifts for her to see someone walking up the steps toward her.

"Leo?" she blurted.

"No," someone answered. The voice was muffled, but Olivia had no trouble hearing what was said. "Move, and I start shooting. And I won't be careful about keeping the shots away from your little boy."

## Chapter Sixteen

Leo's lungs were on fire, and he couldn't catch his breath. Worse, he couldn't see squat, but he forced himself to try to clear his head. To think. To remember what the hell had happened to him.

He felt around and realized he was lying on the grass. Maybe his yard. There was smoke everywhere, along with the stench of burning rubber and gasoline. He was coughing, but so was someone else. He soon realized that someone else was Carter. The ranch hand was on his knees next to Leo, and he was trying to bat away the smoke.

Groaning, Leo tried to sit, but he failed on the first try. His head was throbbing, and he was dizzy, but he'd thankfully managed to hang on to his gun.

"The truck blew up," Carter mumbled in between coughs.

It wasn't easy, but Leo picked through the memories in his spinning head and tried to piece things together. Yeah, there had been some kind of explosion. Maybe one of the firebombs. And it'd indeed

ripped through the front end of the truck. The airbags had deployed. But that wasn't the reason his
head was throbbing.

No.

Leo remembered someone clubbing him.

Who had done that? Bernice maybe? Maybe
someone who'd come up from outside the truck?
He just didn't know, but he sure as hell was about
to figure that out.

*Cameron. Olivia.* Those two names made it
through the blistering pain and the dizziness. Olivia
and Cameron were inside his house, a house that
could be on fire, and he had to get them out.

He cursed, getting to his hands and knees so he
could try to lever himself up and stand. Leo finally
managed it, with Carter's help, but he wasn't sure
he could make it even a step without falling.

"I think Edwin's still in the truck," Carter said,
still coughing. "Wally and some of the other hands
went running over there, I think. I think," he repeated to let Leo he wasn't sure of that at all. "I
need to get Edwin away from the fire."

Damn. Leo hadn't worked his thoughts around
to the ranch hand who'd been in the truck with him,
but now he looked back at the truck. Or rather, what
was left of it. It was about thirty feet away from him,
and the front end was definitely on fire. It was those
flames that were causing the smothering black smoke.

"Go to Edwin," Leo told Carter. "And if Bernice
is still in the truck, get her out, too."

Leo wanted to help, but he had no intention of doing that at Olivia's and Cameron's expense. He needed to get to them, to take them to safety. Heaven knew, though, where that would be right now, but the cruiser was still in the yard. He could get them inside and drive away from the burning truck, away from the house. Maybe then they'd be safe.

Carter hurried in the direction of the truck and disappeared into the curtain of smoke. Leo got moving, too, though each step was an effort. The seconds were just ticking by, and each second was time he needed to rescue Izzie, Olivia and his son.

Leo hadn't even made it to the porch when he heard the footsteps behind him. With his gun aimed as best he could manage, he whirled in that direction. He'd expected to see one of his hands since they'd no doubt be coming to help, but it wasn't.

It was Samuel.

"Don't shoot," the man said, lifting his hands in the air. His breath was gusting and his face was covered with sweat.

"What the hell are you doing here?" Leo snarled, but figured he knew the answer. Samuel was there to try to kill him.

Maybe.

Leo shook his head because that didn't make sense. If Samuel had wanted him dead, he could have shot him in the back. Leo knew with his head injury, he probably wouldn't have even seen it coming.

"I got an anonymous call," Samuel answered. He

was coughing, too, and trying to bat the smoke away from his face. "And the caller said Olivia had been taken hostage, that I was to get here as fast as I could. I had to leave my SUV at the end of the road because of the fire, and I ran the rest of the way here."

Leo wished his head would stop throbbing for just a second so he could figure out if that was the truth. Then, he decided it didn't matter. The only thing that mattered right now was Olivia and Cameron, and he didn't have time to interrogate her father. Or to arrest him.

"Wait here," Leo told him. "I'll deal with you when I get back."

Samuel didn't listen. He was right on Leo's heels as he made his way up the porch steps. "Is Olivia inside? Has she really been taken?" Samuel's two questions ran together, and his panic and fear sure sounded genuine.

*Sounded.*

But Leo wasn't about to take that reaction at face value. Too bad he didn't have any cuffs on him that he could use to restrain Samuel, but he did do a quick frisk of the man. Samuel didn't stop him and voluntarily handed Leo the handgun he'd been wearing in a shoulder holster.

"I need to make sure Olivia and Cameron are okay," Samuel said between his coughs. His breathing sounded more labored than Leo's.

Leo didn't waste time arguing with the man. He bolted into the foyer and glanced around. Olivia wasn't there, but someone had tracked dirt onto the floor. Maybe Carter when Leo had sent the hand in to stay with Olivia.

But the feeling in his gut told him it hadn't been Carter, that it'd been someone with bad intentions.

That got Leo moving faster as he headed for the stairs. Again, Samuel was right behind him.

"I didn't know," Samuel said. "I swear I didn't."

While Leo very much wanted to know what the man meant by that, he didn't respond. "Olivia?" he called out.

He listened for her to answer while he drowned out the other noises. The ranch hands in the yard who were apparently trying to put out the truck fire. He could hear water running, so they were likely using the hose. In the distance, he also heard the wail of sirens. Maybe the ambulance and fire department. Maybe Daniel. But what Leo didn't hear was Olivia.

Leo called out her name again and, despite his blurred vision, he hurried up the stairs. There was some smoke here, too, and the lights were off. But Leo could still see the gun on the floor. The gun that Olivia had no doubt taken from his office closet.

And he could see Olivia.

His heart stopped.

There was Olivia in the dark hall. Not alone. Someone was behind her. And that someone had a gun aimed at her head.

Dragging Samuel with him, Leo automatically ducked for cover behind the wall at the top of the stairs, but he glanced out to see if he had a shot to take out Olivia's captor.

He didn't.

The person was using Olivia as a shield. Hell. Olivia could be killed.

"The caller was right," Samuel declared, and he would have darted from cover if Leo hadn't held him back.

Yeah, the caller was right, and later, Leo would figure out if Olivia's captor had made that call and if Samuel was in on this plan. He didn't appear to be. He seemed to be just as shaken as Leo, but Leo didn't trust the man one bit.

"If you do anything stupid," Leo warned Samuel, "I'll kill you. Understand? You're not going to do anything that'll put Olivia or Cameron in any more danger than they already are."

Samuel must have seen that Leo wasn't bluffing, that he would indeed kill him, because the man quit struggling. Groaning, he sank onto the stairs.

"Help her," Samuel said like a plea. "Help her."

That was the plan. Well, as soon as he had a plan, that would be Leo's top priority. For now he had to figure out what was going on. Since Olivia was obviously a hostage, he had to find out what her captor wanted.

"I'm Deputy Leo Logan," he said, identifying himself. And while he was a thousand percent sure it wouldn't work, he added, "Throw down your weapon."

He couldn't be sure, but he thought the person laughed.

"I'm sorry, Leo," Olivia called out, her voice trembling. "I didn't have a choice."

Hearing her caused so many things to hit Leo at once. Fear—yeah, it was there big-time—and a sickening dread that he'd made a huge mistake by going outside to question Bernice. If he hadn't done that, if he'd stayed put, he would have been inside and stopped this.

Leo glanced out just as Olivia opened her mouth as if to say more, but her captor jammed the gun harder against her head. Leo wanted to rip the person apart when he saw the trickle of blood slide down Olivia's cheek.

"I told her if she didn't throw down the gun," the captor said, "that I'd start shooting."

The rage came like a low, dangerous simmer, and Leo had no doubts that it would soon go full-boil. This SOB had just threatened not only Olivia but also Cameron. The nursery was just two doors down from where Olivia was standing.

Leo pushed everything out of his mind—or rather, tried to do that—to focus on the voice. Not a normal speaking voice. This was a mix of gravel and hoarse whisper. Obviously a ploy to disguise who was speaking. And it was working. Leo didn't know if this was a hired thug or one of their two remaining suspects, Rena and Bernice.

"I was afraid one of the bullets would hit Cameron," Olivia said in a mutter. "So I yelled for Izzie to stay put with him."

Yeah, he was right there with her on this. Like Olivia, he would have done whatever it took to stop someone from firing a gun this close to Cameron. Still would. That meant this couldn't come down to a shooting match even if Olivia could get clear enough for Leo to have a shot.

"Who are you?" Leo asked. "What do you want?"

"I'm leaving with Olivia, and you're going to make sure that happens," her captor readily answered. "I need a vehicle."

"That's your plan?" Leo taunted. "To go driving out of here with Olivia?"

"That's my plan that'll work," the person countered. This time the voice was louder, not so much of a whisper, and Leo was almost certain that it was a woman's voice.

"Is that Bernice or Rena talking?" Leo murmured to Samuel.

The man's head snapped up, the shock in his eyes, which meant he hadn't considered it to be either of them. And maybe it wasn't. After all, it could be a female hired gun.

To give Samuel another chance to listen to the captor's voice, Leo went with another question. "I'll get you the vehicle," he said, "but tell me what you want. Is it money?"

However, before Leo got an answer, someone called out from the bottom floor. "Boss? You okay?"

Wally.

Leo had to make a snap decision. He didn't want to put another person in danger, and that's exactly what would happen if Wally came upstairs. Added to that, it might spook the captor and cause her to start firing.

"Wally, I need a truck brought around to the back of the house," Leo instructed. "Park close to the porch and leave the keys in the ignition."

"Uh, sure. Are you okay?" Wally repeated. Since Wally wasn't an idiot, he knew something was wrong, but hopefully he wouldn't do something to escalate this standoff.

"Tell him to hurry," the captor snapped.

"Hurry," Leo added to Wally and looked back at Olivia. He wished he could do something to ease that terror in her eyes, but the only thing that would make that go away was to get her out of this situation.

"How much money to do you want?" Leo asked the person holding her. "Or are you after some kind of leverage. I'm guessing this is a whole lot more than you wanting me to fix a parking ticket."

"I'll pay whatever you want," Samuel added. "Just name your price."

The person made a strange sound. A snarl dripping with outrage.

"Enough of this!" Olivia's captor spat the words out and before Leo could even react, bashed Olivia on the head.

"Stop!" Leo shouted, trying to take aim. But he

didn't have a shot because the captor dragged Olivia back up and put her in a choke hold.

And that's when he saw the face.

Bernice.

THE PAIN SHOT through Olivia, so fast, so strong, that she wouldn't have been able to stay on her feet had her captor not latched onto her. And was now choking her.

Bernice.

She was trying to kill her.

Olivia didn't know why—not yet—but it had to have something to do with her father. Was that why he was there? Olivia had only caught a glimpse of him, but she'd seen him with Leo.

And Leo had been hurt.

There'd been blood on his head and, while he'd looked formidable, he'd also looked a little dazed. Like her. Mercy. Had her father done that to him?

Olivia somehow managed to catch her breath and jab her elbow into Bernice's stomach. The woman grunted in pain but only dug the barrel of the gun in harder on Olivia's head.

She didn't know where Bernice had gotten the weapon since she knew the ranch hands had frisked her before they'd put her in the truck. But, obviously, she'd managed to get her hands on one.

And would without hesitation use it to kill.

Olivia only hoped she found out why this was happening. She didn't want to die without knowing that, and not without knowing that Leo and Cameron would be safe. If necessary, she'd sacrifice herself for them.

But so would Leo.

In fact, he was no doubt trying to figure out how to get her out of this.

Olivia heard Leo's phone ring. It was in his jeans' pocket, but he didn't answer it. Seconds later, it rang again.

"Let's move," Bernice ordered and practically shoved her forward. Something that Bernice didn't need to do. Olivia desperately wanted to put as much distance as she could between Cameron and Bernice's gun. "If the truck's not there waiting for us, then I start putting bullets in you. Is that what you want, Leo? You want your lover to bleed out in front of you?"

"No." Leo stepped out, much too far, and gave Olivia a quick glance before he fastened his gaze on Bernice. "I'd make a better hostage than Olivia," he proclaimed, attempting to bargain. "Nobody will fire at you if you have me."

"I don't want you." There was so much anger and venom in Bernice's voice.

"But you tried to have me killed," Leo fired back. "That's why you hired Milton. You called him from the estate to tell him to go ahead with the attack."

Bernice certainly didn't deny that, and with her grip still tight on Olivia's neck, they moved forward a few more steps. "I wanted Olivia arrested," Bernice spelled out. "I wanted her in jail."

"For Samuel," Leo stated. Unlike Bernice's, his voice was nearly calm now, but there was a dangerous cop's edge to it. Like a rattler ready to strike. "You did all of this for him, didn't you?"

"Did you?" her father asked. He moved out from cover, too. "God, Bernice. Did you do this for me?"

Bernice wasn't so quick to answer this time. "Yes, and you repaid me by getting back together with Rena. I would have done anything for you. *Anything.*" She emphasized the word, sounding more than a little frantic. "And you kept throwing that gold-digging bimbo in my face."

Olivia thought of Rena and wondered if the woman was still alive. Maybe Bernice had taken care of her before she'd come here. Clearly, this was a last-ditch mission to finish what she'd started. A mission that had left two dead. Possibly even more.

"I'll go with you, Bernice," Samuel offered. He stepped even farther out, too far now to dive back to cover if Bernice fired at him. "Leave Olivia, and I'll go with you. We can get out of the country, some place that doesn't have extradition."

Olivia sucked in a breath. Held it. She knew there was no way her father would actually do that. This was a ploy to try to free her, and she welcomed it. Not because she thought it would work, but because he might be able to at least distract Bernice while Leo and she did something.

"Move down the stairs now," Bernice ordered Leo and Samuel. "No stupid tricks, either, or I'll start firing. I know where the nursery is. I heard when the nanny answered Olivia, and that's where I'll aim the shots."

Olivia was close enough now to see the look in Leo's eyes. The rage. She felt the same. How could this witch threaten their son like that? And all because she had wrongly believed that Samuel owed her something. Maybe owed her love. Well, Olivia wasn't going to let Bernice take away the people she loved.

Leo and her father walked backward down the stairs, each of them watching every move that Bernice and she were making. Olivia tried to calculate the best place for her to make a stand—whatever that stand would be, though, she didn't know. Not yet. But if she could just get Bernice out of the house, then it might lessen the risk for Cameron.

It would increase her own risk, though. Because there was no way Bernice would keep her alive once she'd finished using her as a shield.

"Bernice," Samuel tried again. "Please stop this."

"Shut up," she snapped. "Leo, you'd better tell your ranch hands to back off once we're outside."

"Hear that, Wally?" Leo said, and from the corner of her eye, Olivia saw the man in the foyer. He was still armed, but like Leo, he didn't have a safe shot. "Let the other hands know to back off."

With his eyes wide, Wally nodded and took out his phone. "Daniel's at the end of the road," he relayed. "He's walking up now. Said he tried to call you but that you didn't answer your phone."

So that's who had been trying to get in touch with Leo. Good. Daniel was a smart lawman. He might be able to lie in wait and do something to stop Bernice.

The moment Bernice had Olivia on the bottom floor, the woman started moving her through the open living room and into the kitchen. Olivia kept her attention focused on Leo, looking for any signs of what they could do. He seemed steady. Determined. And he was watching every step that Bernice took.

Olivia wished the woman would trip but then rethought that. Bernice's first instinct might be to pull the trigger, and they were literally right below the nursery.

Bernice's hold finally loosened as Olivia felt the woman reach behind her. She heard the rattle of the doorknob as Bernice unlocked the door and used her elbow to push it open.

Olivia immediately felt the rush of the still hot summer air. Air tainted with the stench of smoke. She prayed that the hands had been able to put out the fire so that it couldn't spread to the house.

"The truck's waiting for you," Leo said.

Because Bernice quickly regained her choke hold, Olivia couldn't see the truck, but she could hear the engine running. Could also hear some muffled conversation, no doubt from the hands.

Bernice's arms were already tense, the muscles knotted to the point where it had to be painful. Olivia hoped she was in pain anyway. Hoped that her pain would get a whole lot worse before this was over. Olivia wanted the woman to pay for all the misery she'd caused.

Muttering obscenities, Bernice stepped onto the porch and immediately shifted Olivia to the side. No doubt so that she could check out the truck while keeping an eye on Leo and Samuel.

"Bernice, if you do this, I'll kill you," her father said. He was practically shoulder to shoulder with Leo as they slowly made their way to the porch. Leo still had hold of his gun, and her father's hands were balled into fists.

Olivia felt Bernice's muscles tighten even more. "No, you won't kill me," Bernice snapped like a challenge. "Because I'll kill you first."

Bernice shifted the gun, obviously trying to aim it at her father. Leo brought up his weapon, too, and in that split second, Olivia knew she had to do something to stop Bernice from killing them both.

With the adrenaline slamming through her, Olivia threw her weight against Bernice, ramming her body into the woman's. It worked. Bernice started to fall backward.

But she took Olivia with her.

Olivia's head bashed against the porch floor and the two of them tumbled down the steps together.

Just as Bernice pulled the trigger.

## Chapter Seventeen

Leo shouted for Bernice to stop, but he knew it wouldn't do any good. Nor could he get to Olivia in time. He was running toward the women as they fell.

And as the shot blasted through the air.

He refused to think that the shot had hit Olivia. Refused to believe that she could be hurt or dead.

Bernice was definitely alive, though. Despite the fall, the woman tried to aim her gun at him. Leo did something about that. He kicked it out of her hand. The gun went flying and he didn't bother to look where it landed. He gave Bernice a kick, too, right in her face, and the woman wailed, falling back into the yard.

Leo kept his eye on Bernice, but he took hold of Olivia's arm and pulled her back onto the porch. That was a risk, since moving her could aggravate her injuries, but he needed to get her away from Bernice.

He cursed when he saw the blood on Olivia's face. Blood on her shirt, too, and she was moaning in pain. Maybe from a gunshot wound, or maybe just from the wounds she'd gotten in the fall.

"Check on Cameron," Leo called out to no one in particular, but he knew one of his hands would do that. After all, the shot Bernice had fired could have gone into the nursery.

"Help Olivia," Leo added to Samuel as he readied himself to ease her out of his arms so he could jump down in the yard and deal with Bernice.

But Samuel beat him to it.

Samuel rushed past him, barreling down the steps and snatching up Bernice's gun. He dropped to his knees and in the same motion grabbed on to the woman's hair, dragging her head off the ground.

He put the gun to the center of Bernice's forehead.

"Any last words before I kill you?" Samuel asked. Of course, there was emotion in his voice.

The wrong kind of emotion.

Not anger or fear from what had just happened. This was an icy-cold hatred that Leo knew could cause the man to commit murder. And that's exactly what it would be if he pulled the trigger now and shot an unarmed woman. Leo couldn't let her life end like this.

"Samuel," Leo said, keeping his tone as calm as he could manage. "We need to help Olivia. We have to make sure Cameron is okay."

"Any last words before I kill you?" Samuel repeated, shouting the words at Bernice.

The woman's face was covered with blood, and

her nose was likely broken, but she still managed to look defiant. "I loved you," Bernice told him. "And you betrayed me. Go ahead. Kill me. Then, you'll have to live with that for the rest of your life."

A life Samuel might spend behind bars if he actually pulled the trigger. Leo didn't care much for the man, but he didn't want things to end like this.

"Dad…" Olivia murmured, her soft voice carrying over the sound of the truck engine and Samuel's ragged breaths. "Let Leo arrest her. Bernice will spend every day she's got left in a cage."

A hoarse sob broke from Samuel's throat, but he kept the gun in place. "I believe Bernice killed your mother. I think she gave Simone those drugs that made her wreck the car. She could have killed you."

Bernice certainly didn't deny any of that. Just the opposite. "I did what I needed to do."

And there it was. The confession that Olivia had no doubt waited years to hear.

Keeping watch on Bernice and Samuel, Leo slipped his arm around Olivia and helped her get to her feet. She practically sagged against him, but considering everything that'd happened, she was a lot steadier than he'd thought she would be.

"I stopped Simone from divorcing you and taking your daughter," Bernice told Samuel. There was the same cold rage in her voice now that had been in Samuel's. "I would have done the same to stop Olivia from taking Cameron from you."

So, that was her motive. It turned Leo's blood

to ice to think that Bernice had nearly gotten away with it.

Leo spotted Daniel peering around corner of the house, but motioned for his brother to stay back. With Samuel still armed, Leo didn't want him getting spooked and shooting Bernice.

"Dad, you need to put down your gun," Olivia tried again. "We don't want any more shots fired. It could scare Cameron."

Leo finally saw something he wanted to see. Samuel pulled back the gun. It was still aimed at Bernice, but was no longer pressed to her forehead.

"I want her dead," Samuel said, his shoulders shaking with his sobs. "I want her to pay."

"And she will," Leo assured him. Since he wasn't sure Olivia could stay standing without his support, he motioned for Daniel to move in. "My brother will take Bernice into custody. She'll be charged with murder, murder for hire and a whole bunch of other charges. Olivia was right about her spending the rest of her life in a cage."

"As if I care," Bernice snarled, still challenging Samuel with her fierce stare. "Go ahead and kill me." She smiled, a sick smile given the blood trickling out of her mouth.

"Bernice wants to die by your hand," Olivia told her father. "That way, she can keep on punishing you because you'll have to come to terms with what's gone on here. She wants you to suffer. Make her suffer instead."

That finally seemed to get through to Samuel. He leaned away from Bernice and sat back on the ground. Daniel moved in closer, reached down and took the gun from Samuel's hand.

"You were supposed to kill me!" Bernice shouted, darting glances around the yard. "It wasn't supposed to end like this."

Daniel ignored her shouts, hauled Bernice up and slapped a pair of plastic cuffs on her wrists.

Leo didn't want to give the woman another moment of his attention, nor did he want to keep Olivia outside. He turned to lead Olivia back inside so they could check on Cameron. And so he could see how bad her injuries were. However, before he could do that, Wally came hurrying out.

"Cameron and the nanny are fine," Wally said. "Not a scratch on them."

This time Leo thought Olivia sagged from relief as she went into his arms and buried her face against Leo's neck. "He's okay. Our baby's okay."

Yeah, and Leo felt a mountain of relief of his own. Bernice hadn't done her worst. She hadn't managed to hurt their son.

"I would have killed her had she hurt Cameron," Samuel said, looking up at them. He moved closer and sank onto the bottom porch step. He looked exhausted and beaten down. Like a man who'd lost way too much and might not recover from those losses.

Considering their past, Leo was surprised that he felt any sympathy for Samuel. But he did. It had to be hard coming to terms with the fact that he'd been living under the same roof with his wife's killer.

"I told Izzie to stay put until you got up there," Wally said, breaking the silence. "Didn't figure you'd want Cameron out here. Also didn't figure you'd want him to see Olivia and you like this, all covered with blood."

They were, indeed, covered with blood, and Wally was right. Leo didn't want Cameron anywhere near Bernice.

Leo pulled back and took a moment to examine Olivia. There was a gash on her head that needed tending, and from what he could tell, that's where most of the blood had come from. Still, she'd need to go the hospital.

"The truck fire's out," Wally told them a moment later, giving Leo yet more good news. Wally tipped his head to Bernice. "You want me to help Daniel get her out of here?"

Leo definitely wanted that. "Yeah. Bring the cruiser to the backyard and see if Carter or one of the other hands can go through every inch of the house to make sure it's secure. And call for an ambulance," Leo added.

"It's already here," Daniel supplied. "Well, it's nearby anyway. The fire department's putting out the flames on the road, and the ambulance can get up here then. We might need two ambulances, though. Edwin's hurt. So is Rena. I found her trying to crawl through the pasture to get to the road."

Leo certainly hadn't forgotten about Rena, but she wasn't a high priority for him now. Obviously, though, she was for Samuel.

"How bad is she hurt?" he asked.

Daniel shrugged and kept his hand clamped around Bernice's arm. "Not sure. But I don't think she has a lot of injuries. She seemed drugged to me."

"That bimbo was supposed to die in a car crash like Simone," Bernice snarled.

So that's what had happened to Rena. It would add another count of attempted murder to the charges that would be filed against Bernice.

"The idiot I hired to steal the journals from Olivia's house was going to doctor them," Bernice added, "to make it look as if Simone was afraid Rena would kill her."

It wouldn't have worked since Olivia had made copies of the journal pages, but Bernice obviously hadn't known that. That also meant burning down Olivia's house had been all for nothing.

Bernice glanced around the yard again, putting Leo on alert. He eased Olivia behind him and readied his gun in case there was about to be another attack.

"I think she's looking for her hired thug," Daniel said, his voice as calm as a lake. "When I was walking up the road, and before I spotted Rena, I caught some guy hiding in a ditch. According to his driver's license, his name is Frank Sutton. I cuffed him, and a couple of the hands are guarding him until I can get back down there."

Bernice made a sound of outrage and tried to ram her body into Daniel's. Daniel just slung her around and yanked back her arms.

"Guess Bernice isn't too happy about losing the last of her lackeys," Daniel commented.

"You're sure he's the last one?" Olivia asked.

"Yeah," Daniel confirmed. "Sutton was pretty chatty and got even chattier when I mentioned that the first to make a full confession would be the one to get a lighter sentence. I didn't bother to tell him that the lighter sentence would just be taking the death penalty off the table, so the guy prattled on. He claims that Bernice hired him to attach a firebomb to underside of the truck when the hands drove down to check on her."

Leo hadn't spotted anyone doing that, but it would have been possible. The guy could have used the ditch for cover and sneaked out of it when the hands had been talking to Bernice.

In the distance, Leo finally heard the ambulance sirens coming closer. It wouldn't be long before they arrived and he could get Olivia the medical help she needed.

Carter and another ranch hand came out from the side of the house, heading straight to Daniel in case he needed help with Bernice, but Leo thought his brother had it under control. Better yet, Leo no longer had that feeling in his gut that something was wrong. For the first time since this all began, he thought the danger might finally be over.

"You took a risk putting a firebomb in the truck and having it go off while you were in it," Leo pointed out to Bernice just as Wally pulled the cruiser into the backyard.

Bernice clammed up. Probably because she didn't want to fill in any blanks for them. But apparently her lackey had already done that.

"According to our chatty *friend*, Frank Sutton, the firebomb didn't have much juice," Daniel explained. "Just enough to mess up the front of the truck and create a distraction."

A distraction that Bernice had used to her advantage. It'd helped, too, that she'd known it was coming and had been ready to bash Edwin and Leo.

"How'd Bernice get in the house?" Olivia asked.

Again, it wasn't Bernice who answered but Carter, just as Daniel and the ranch hand stuffed Bernice into the back seat of the cruiser.

"Edwin told me that Bernice grabbed his gun," Carter explained, "and she bashed both him and you on the head when the airbags deployed."

Leo hadn't needed to be told about the head bashing part. He had a knot on his temple, and it was throbbing badly. Still, he'd been lucky that his injuries hadn't been a whole lot worse.

"How's Edwin?" Leo asked Carter.

"Fine. He might need a couple of stitches. You might need some, too," Carter added, giving Leo the once-over. "You want me to ride with your brother to the sheriff's office?"

"Sure." Though Leo figured with Bernice cuffed, she wasn't much of a threat. Still, it wouldn't hurt to have a little overkill, considering the woman was a murderer.

"One more thing," Leo said before Daniel could get behind the wheel of the cruiser. "Did Sutton mention who killed Randall?"

Daniel huffed. "He volunteered that it was Bernice, that she'd tried to rile up Randall to get him to kill you, but then he figured out what she'd done. He says Bernice killed Randall and got him to dispose of the body. He claims it was Bernice's idea to use a Sycamore Grove SUV because she intended to set up Rena."

Leo gave that some thought. "You think Sutton is the one who killed him?" he proposed.

"That'd be my guess," Daniel answered.

Leo nearly added for Daniel to push getting that info during interrogations, but knew his brother would do that without the reminder. Besides, even if Bernice hadn't been the one to pull the trigger that'd killed Randall, she'd still go down for his murder.

"Come on," Leo said, slipping his arm around Olivia again. "Let me take you to the front to the ambulance."

She stopped, held her ground and stared up at him. "I don't want to go to the hospital. *Please*. I don't want to leave Cameron."

It wasn't the *please* that got to him. It was the

look on her face. Not pain or panic. Just a mountain of concern for her child.

"All right," he agreed. "We'll have the EMTs check you, but if they say you should be in the hospital, then you will be." He kissed her to try to soften the order he'd given her. "I'm not going to risk losing you."

"You shouldn't risk losing her," he heard someone say. "Olivia loves you."

Leo was surprised those words had come from Samuel. Sighing, her father got to his feet, walked closer to them and gave Leo a pat on the arm. It felt awkward coming from Samuel, but it was a helluva lot better than the verbal jabs he'd given Leo in the past.

"I'm sorry," Samuel said, his gaze moving to Olivia. "I swear, before tonight, I didn't know it was Bernice who'd killed your mother."

She hesitated as if, Leo presumed, trying to gauge if that were true. She must have decided it was because she nodded.

"If I could fix things between us, I would," Samuel added and then turned to walk away.

"Wait," Olivia said, causing him to stop in his tracks. "Why do you think I'm in love with Leo?"

Leo tensed because he sure as hell didn't want to hear Olivia say that her father had it all wrong, that it wasn't true.

"Because you are," Samuel simply said. "And he's in love with you."

Obviously, that stunned both Olivia and him into

silence because neither confirmed nor denied it. They just stood there, waiting for Samuel to leave. He did. Not through the house, though. Instead, he went in the direction of the front yard. Hopefully, one of the EMTs would check him out, as well.

"I want to hate him," Olivia muttered. There were tears shimmering in her eyes when she turned back to him. "But right now, I'm just so tired of the hate. I'm ready for that being-in-love part."

That sounded...well, hopeful, and despite his throbbing head, Leo found himself smiling. And kissing her. He'd intended it to be a quick reassurance, but it turned into something longer. Deeper. And hotter. The kind of kiss that could land them in bed—if they hadn't been so banged up, that is.

"You're in love with me," he said when they finally broke for air. "And if you're not, then—"

"I'm in love with you," Olivia verified.

Smiling, and then wincing because the smile must have caused her face to hurt, she kissed him. And, yeah, it was one of those long, deep hot ones that made Leo forget all about such things as pain and injuries.

"If you're not in love with me," she said after she'd just rocked his world with a third kiss, "then—"

He stopped her with a fourth kiss. "I'm in love with you," he assured her.

Leo used the fifth kiss to show her just how much.

\* \* \* \* \*

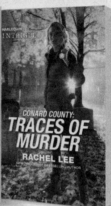

## #2043 PURSUED BY THE SHERIFF
*Mercy Ridge Lawmen* • by Delores Fossen
The bullet that rips through Sheriff Jace Castillo's body stalls his investigation. But being nursed back to health by the shooter's sister is his biggest complication yet. Linnea Martell has always been—and still is—off-limits. And the danger only intensifies when Linnea gets caught in the line of fire...

## #2044 DISAPPEARANCE AT DAKOTA RIDGE
*Eagle Mountain: Search for Suspects* • by Cindi Myers
When Lauren Baker's sister-in-law and niece go missing, she immediately has a suspect in mind and heads to Eagle Mountain, where she turns to Deputy Shane Ellis for help. And when another woman seen with her family is found dead, their desperate pursuit for answers becomes even more urgent.

## #2045 COWBOY IN THE CROSSHAIRS
*A North Star Novel Series* • by Nicole Helm
After attempting to expose corruption throughout the military, former navy SEAL Nate Averly becomes an assassin's next target. When he flees to his brother's Montana ranch, North Star agent Elsie Rogers must protect him and uncover the threat before more lives are lost. But they're up against a cunning adversary who's deadlier than they ever imagined...

## #2046 DISAVOWED IN WYOMING
*Fugitive Heroes: Topaz Unit* • by Juno Rushdan
Fleeing from a CIA kill squad, former operative Dean Delgado finds himself back in Wyoming and befriending veterinarian Kate Sawyer—the woman he was once forced to leave behind. But when an emergency call brings Kate under fire, protecting her is the only mission that matters to Dean—even if it puts his own life at risk.

## #2047 LITTLE GIRL GONE
*A Procedural Crime Story* • by Amanda Stevens
Special agent Thea Lamb returns to her hometown to search for a child whose disappearance echoes a twenty-eight-year-old cold case—her twin sister's abduction. Working with her former partner, Jake Stillwell, Thea must overcome the pain that has tormented her for years. For both Thea and Jake, the job always came first...until now.

## #2048 CHASING THE VIOLET KILLER
by R. Barri Flowers
After witnessing a serial killer murder her relative live on video chat, Secret Service agent Naomi Lincoln is determined to solve the case. But investigating forces her to work with detective Dylan Hester—the boyfriend she left brokenhearted years ago. Capturing the Violet Killer will be the greatest challenge of their lives—especially once he sets his sights on Naomi.

HICNM1221

"If need be, I could run my way out of these woods. You can't
run," Linnea added.

"No, but I can return fire if we get into trouble," Jace argued.
"And I stand a better chance of hitting a target than you do."

It was a good argument. Well, it would have been if he
hadn't had the gunshot wound. It wasn't on his shooting arm,
thank goodness, but he was weak, and any movement could
cause that wound to open up.

"You could bleed out before I get you out of these woods,"
Linnea reminded him. "Besides, I'm not sure you can shoot,
much less shoot straight. You can't even stand up without help."

As if to prove her wrong, he picked up his gun from the
nightstand and straightened his posture, pulling back his
shoulders.

And what little color he had drained from his face.

Cursing him and their situation, she dragged a chair closer
to the window and had him sit down.

"The main road isn't that far, only about a mile," she
continued. Linnea tried to tamp down her argumentative tone.
"I can get there on the ATV and call for help. Your deputies and

the EMTs can figure out the best way to get you to a hospital."

That was the part of her plan that worked. What she didn't feel comfortable about was leaving Jace alone while she got to the main road. Definitely not ideal, but they didn't have any other workable solutions.

Of course, this option wouldn't work until the lightning stopped. She could get through the wind and rain, but if she got struck by lightning or a tree falling from a strike, it could be fatal. First to her, and then to Jace, since he'd be stuck here in the cabin.

He looked up at her, his color a little better now, and his eyes were hard and intense. "I can't let you take a risk like that. Gideon could ambush you."

"That's true," she admitted. "But the alternative is for us to wait here. Maybe for days until you're strong enough to ride out with me. That might not be wise since I suspect you need antibiotics for your wound before an infection starts brewing."

His jaw tightened, and even though he'd had plenty trouble standing, Jace got up. This time he didn't stagger, but she did notice the white-knuckle grip he had on his gun. "We'll see how I feel once the storm has passed."

In other words, he would insist on going with her. Linnea sighed. Obviously, Jace had a mile-wide stubborn streak and was planning on dismissing her *one workable option*.

"If you're hungry, there's some canned soup in the cabinet," she said, shifting the subject.

Jace didn't respond to that. However, he did step in front of her as if to shield her. And he lifted his gun.

"Get down," Jace ordered. "Someone's out there."

*Don't miss*
Pursued by the Sheriff
*by Delores Fossen, available January 2022 wherever Harlequin Intrigue books and ebooks are sold.*

Harlequin.com